A SELKIE'S MAGIC

**The Selkies Heart
Book 1**

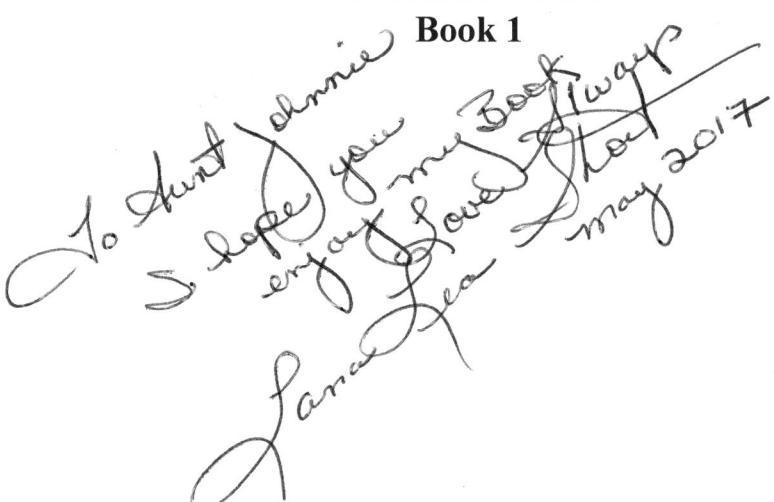

Lana Lea Short

Copyright

ISBN-13: 978-1541268616

ISBN-10: 154126861X

Published 2016, Lana Lea Short. All rights reserved. No part of this publication may be reproduced, stored in a retrieval system, or transmitted in any form or by any means, electronic, mechanical, recording or otherwise, without the prior written permission of the author.

This is a work of fiction. The characters, incidents, and dialogues in this book are the author's imagination and are not to be construed as real. Any resemblance to actual events or persons, living or dead, is completely coincidental.

Dedication

This is for you, Mom, for always being there for me and believing I could fulfill my dreams, even though you were a little worried about how much time I spent in front of the computer.

To my loving and understanding husband John, who always keeps me laughing.

To my editor Ansley Blackstock, words cannot express my gratitude for her expertise in polishing my manuscript.

Acknowledgements

To my wonderful beta readers, Stephen Jacobi, Melesia Lawson Tully, Lydia Williams and Deanna Lang, who made helpful suggestions, encouraged me and believed I was on the right track. You guys are the best, thanks for all your time and work.

A Selkie Song

Author Unknown

An Earthly nurse sits and sings,

And aye, she sings by lily wean, and little ken I by Bairn's father,

Far less the land where he dwells in,

For he came one night to her bed feet, and a grumbly guest, I am sure was he,

Saying "Here am I, they bairns father,

Although I be not comely, I am a man upon the land,

I am a selkie on the sea, And when I'm far and far frae land,

my home it is in Sule Skerrie:"

And he had ta'en a purse of gold, And he had placed it upon her knew,

Saying: "Give it to my little young son,

And take thee up they nurse's fee."

"And it shall come to pass on a summer's day,

When the sun shires bright on every stane

I'll come and fetch my little son, and teach him how to swim the faem."

"And ye shall marry a gunner good, and a right fine gunner I'm sure he'll be,

And the very first shot that he e'er shoots, will kill both my young son and me."

Prologue

1960

The Selkie swam into his undersea cave that contained his human clothing. Last evening he'd had a vision he would find his life mate in the area above the sea caves. He needed to find her as his vision was too strong to disregard. She was a well-built, sturdy young Scot lass with sparkling green eyes and long dark auburn hair which flowed to her waist. He had seen her in his dream, dancing at the local Highland gathering. The young woman in his dreams was Mackenzie Sutherland's destiny.

He strode into the clan gathering and saw her doing the Highland fling with her kilt and hair whipping around her tight young body. Her smile flashed as she moved to the intricate steps of her dance. Her cheeks flushed and her eyes blazed with a heat which drew him like a moth to a flame. Around and around she swirled and kicked to the music of the bagpipes. As she spun around, he could see her beautiful long legs and the sweet curve of her rounded bottom. Her waist, he realized he could circle with his hands. Her bust was full and appeared to be a plump handful. Her complexion was pale as peaches he'd read about in books from her world. While he enjoyed her dance, passion heated his blood, and Mackenzie recognized she was the young woman from his dream.

*****

Skye loved the dancing and the way she felt as the men's eyes remained on her. In her young girl's mind, she understood the power she held over them. She viewed the young dark-haired stranger who watched her with a lustful gleam in his eye. He was a large virile man who possessed a strength about him.

He was the most handsome man she had ever seen and he was considerably taller than the men in her village. His jet-black hair was long and hung down his back in shining silken waves. His eyes were deep brown like the whiskey her father drank. His skin was smooth and tan. His body was hard and taut with muscles which were used to hard work. He bore broad shoulders, which tapered down to a narrow waist and a flat belly.

It was his wicked smile that did her in and made her heart beat wildly beneath her breast. Skye was not so young at sixteen to not know what would be on his mind. Her body and her mind were thinking similar thoughts to his, but without the experience he understood. The closest Skye had ever come to experience, were the naughty books she'd read, which her father had left hidden under the cushion of his favorite overstuffed chair. As Skye glanced at the tall, long-haired man she was sure he knew what to do with those forbidden desires.

Chapter 1

2002
Aileana

As families go, Aileana thought of hers as normal—whatever that may mean. Her family always took their summer vacations in Durness in the Northwestern Highlands of Scotland. Her *seanmhair*, which is Gaelic for grandmother, name was Skye Sutherland, her father's mother. Skye lived in a converted crofter cottage on the rim of the cliffs above the sea. The cottage was constructed of the same stone as the low walls near the cottage. She'd always loved going back each year to her father's childhood home. The Highlands of Scotland were more than the five thousand three hundred and thirty-three miles from Aileana's home in Woodland Hills, a suburb of Los Angeles, California. There were no malls and no traffic, no housing tracts in the Highlands—only the beautiful green hills and cliffs above the sea.

Staying at her *seanmhair's* home above the sea had always been her favorite place to be. She loved to explore the area on her own and enjoyed hiking the sea cliffs and checking out the seashore to see what treasures she might find in her wanderings.

Her sister Adaira was two years younger. She would sometimes join Aileana in her daily adventures, but Adaira showed little interest in exploring the Highlands or the seashore. Adaira spent most of her time in the village with her girlfriends.

The summer of Aileana's fourteenth birthday, she encountered someone special. His name was Kendrick Morgan, they met by chance.

As she walked along the shore looking out to the rocks beyond the surf, she noticed a raft of seals swimming among the towering quartzite pillars. The seals were so sleek and agile as they glided through the waves near the rocks. The seals watched her with big soulful eyes so full of mischief as she ambled along the shore.

It made her wish she'd brought her shortboard from home. She realized the surf here was not as good as up the coast in Thurso, which had an awesome right-hand break. Still, she thought it would have been wonderful to jump on her stick and paddle out and sun herself among the seals.

On one of her daily hikes, Aileana came across a small sea cave, which in itself was not a big a deal. The area around Durness was known for a big sea grotto called Smoo Cave. The cavern was the important tourist attraction of this area. The small fissure, she found, was not too far down the beach from her *seanmhair's* home.

Her *seanmhair's* cottage was near Durness and about ten miles from Cape Wrath. As she came up to the small sea cave she noticed a young man coming from the mouth of the cave.

She was ever the friendly So Cal surfer type, so she waved hello and said, "Hey, dude. What's up?"

He was tall and lean and well-built, narrow hips and a broad chest. His sculpted body was smooth and sleek without hair except on his head. Talk about a six-pack; he had an eight pack going on, and he took her breath away. Taking Aileana's breath away was no easy feat, coming from the area she lived in. You could see rock stars and gorgeous hunky actors almost daily on Ventura Blvd. His eyes were the color of dark obsidian and his ink-black hair fell to the middle of his back. She thought he must be in a rock band or something like that. His skin was tan and wet from swimming in the sea. He possessed a wonderful smile that showed his perfect bright white teeth. His deep voice was smooth as honey with a warm, welcoming Scottish brogue.

"Hello," he replied.

His full name was Kendrick Broden Morgan. Kendrick told her he lived in the area and enjoyed swimming here with his friends. Aileana asked where his friends were. This new acquaintance told her that they had left earlier before she got to the beach. Kendrick inquired what her name was, and she said, "Aileana Sutherland."

"Ye have a strange way of talking. Where are ye from?"

"I'm from an area near Los Angeles, California."

"American? What brings ye here to Scotland?"

"Yeah, I'm American, but my family roots are here. My *seanmhair* lives up on the cliffs close by. My dad was a local guy."

"What took your da to California? Is he the forgotten Beach Boy?"

She laughed and said, "Dad moved away after college. An ocean research company near Malibu recruited him."

Kendrick and Aileana met each day for the rest of the week; they talked and swam in the ocean. He told her about his family, he was the second son in a family of five siblings. He had an older brother named Callum who was busy learning how to take over his father's job. His youngest brother was Duncan, a wild and rebellious fellow who liked to see how far he could push the limits of his father's patience. Kendrick also had two sisters. His older sister was Sorcha, she was married and had a family of her own. His younger sister Ceana worked in the village and still lived with her parents. He told her about his parents, who were so in love that they acted as if they were still newlyweds. He said someday he hoped he would be lucky and find that type of love his parents enjoyed. He told her that he worked in town part-time and part-time for his father.

On the last day of that week, Aileana's flight back to California was to depart late in the evening. They met in the morning by the sea cave again. And it was then Kendrick gave her a beautiful pink pearl. The pearl was in the shape of a teardrop and had the most amazing luster. It was about the size of an almond. He told her this was to remember their friendship and time together.

Aileana thought, *Like I would ever forget him, not likely.*

Chapter 2

2014
Finman

The Finman was out beyond the breakers watching the humans as they sailed close to the shore. The humans had no way of knowing he was so close; they were not even aware of his clan's existence.

The humans have told stories of the Finfolk since the beginning of time. They were a race of dark and gloomy sorcerers, feared and mistrusted by mortals. But as time passed, the humans believed the stories to be only ancient folk tales.

It was now the time for him to take what he wanted. He needed to capture some humans to sell to his Finfolk brothers. There were some in his clan who didn't want the trouble of hunting down the humans.

He reveled in the thrill of the hunt, more than most of the clan, which made him one of the master hunters. Beside the silver he would collect from selling his captives; he needed a new female to warm his bed. His last bed slave decided to throw herself off the cliffs of his home on the island of Hildaland. Besides killing herself and depriving him of her sex, she also took his future heir with her.

Not that he cared she died; he had planned on selling her after the birth of his heir. She was too fragile of a human; she barely survived the pounding his body gave her as he undertook impregnating her. These human females made better slaves than wives, he thought. He still needed more male heirs to ensure he maintained a controlling hand on his clan. The Finman knew there was power in numbers where his clan was concerned.

He swam toward the sailboat to get a better view of the humans on board the vessel. He counted four males and two females. He summoned his malicious sorcerer's magic from deep in his black heart, to raise up a storm. He sent out his power to create a wall of black clouds and a torrential downpour of rain. He wanted to see what havoc it would create for the sailboat. His booming laughter sounded like thunder. He watched the humans struggle with the sails. He viewed his destruction taking place. The Finman observed one of the females get hit with the mainsail boom as it swung around knocking her into the sea.

He started to close in on his prey but became aware of a Seelie presence. What in the name of all that is unholy would a Seelie be doing here? As he watched where the female went into the water, he noticed a Selkie nudging the unconscious female to the surface. The Selkie then removed his skin of fur and swam to the shore with the female. The Selkie carried her to the beach and laid the female on the shore.

He watched as the huge muscular Selkie slowly left the beach as the females' companions made their way down the shore toward her motionless form. His anger grew with every moment he watched the humans help the female. He was unsuccessful in his hunt. The large, dark Selkie would pay for seizing his prey. He had neither a sex slave nor a male slave to sell this day. He would not fail the next time he went to hunt.

Chapter 3

2014
Kendrick

Kendrick came up out of the sea and stood upon the land. Saltwater dripped down the long length of his hair. There were rivulets of seawater trickling all the way down his body. He came to the shore along the northern coast of Scotland in an area well known by his Selkie Clan. He left his skin of fur out on the towering quartzite pillars that rose up out of the sea, well hidden among the creags. He walked to the concealed small sea cave close to the shore, hidden by large boulders. Within the cave, he kept a change of clothes to wear when not in his Selkie form.

Kendrick walked to the land where the hills were so abundant and the new fresh grass smelled so sweet. He came to the land to find the woman who'd mesmerized him with the haunting green eyes last evening. He'd been swimming in his Selkie form during the late summer storm the past evening. With eyes that could see through the darkness, he viewed the sailboat with the humans on board. Kendrick watched them struggle with the sails when the storm came upon them.

The humans were out sailing in the early evening on a fair-sized sailboat. The evening was quite chilly, even for August. He saw a beautiful auburn-haired woman heading toward the aft deck before one of the men yelled, "There are storm clouds up ahead, come back up to the cockpit!"

There, dead ahead, less than two hundred yards away, was a black wall of clouds, and a deluge of rain pouring down. The young woman had barely grabbed the cockpit rail before the boat was buried in water up to the lifelines.

The boat was then at a twenty to thirty-degree angle. The storm hit so unexpectedly that there was no time to lower the jib or mainsail. She ended up standing straight up on the seatback on the opposite side the cockpit holding on for dear life to the shroud lines around her, looking straight down at the rough, churning, dark water. If the boat capsized the shroud lines would pull her down. It would have been nearly impossible for her friends to see her on the deck. No chance with the waves washing over the bow and the rain coming down in pounding sheets. Without warning, the boom swung around and caught her square in the back and knocked her overboard. Her shipmates didn't notice the young beauty fall into the sea.

Kendrick swam to her and pulled her from the dark writhing sea. He swam with her and also held his Selkie pelt, which he removed from his body as he needed his human form to take her from the sea. Kendrick swam with her to shore and placed her limp body on the sand. He stayed until her shipmates called out to her on the shore where she now lay.

While Kendrick swam with her to the shore, he had pushed her hair away from her face so he was able to drink in more of her beauty. As her hair came away from her face and neck, he noticed a gold chain around her neck that lay between her breasts. On that chain was a single large pink teardrop pearl. The young woman who wore the beautiful pearl, given in friendship long ago, was the bonnie young lass, his Aileana.

Out in the water, Kendrick could see her as she came to. He was aware she heard her friends call her name. After much coughing and trying to catch her breath, she called out to her friends. They ran up the beach to see if she was okay. They all started to talk at once about what happened.

He had stayed just beyond the breakers to watch. He wasn't able to hear what the humans spoke of, but he was able to tell by their body movements that Aileana had started to become lucid again.

She was a beautiful young woman with hair a rich dark auburn that flowed to her waist in soft curls. Even soaking wet and looking like she'd been washed ashore with the sea kelp, she was still exquisite. Her plump lips just begged to be kissed; any male would lose himself kissing those lips. Her lightly tanned skin had a light sprinkling of freckles across the bridge of her nose. She had the build of a woman who swam and the firm young muscles of a person who spent time being physically active. She was small and compact, but very curvaceous. She was a woman any Selkie male would want to have in his bed.

Chapter 4

Aileana

Yesterday's storm had come without warning. So Aileana checked with the local weather channel and made sure there would be no storms for today. She'd brought her shortboard with her from California since she knew she'd be in Scotland at least a year. Aileana would take the stick out and at least float out beyond the breakers if there were no waves. It was a warmish day for Northern Scotland, but definitely not the kind of summer day she was used to in Southern California. That was okay with her; Aileana would just wear her steamer. She'd known her winter wetsuit would come in handy while in Scotland.

She waxed up her stick and put the leash around her ankle out of habit. She certainly didn't think the board would be getting away from her today; the surf was all "ankle busters."

Aileana ran with the board and jumped into the surf, landing on the board belly down. She paddled to the outside break to see if she could catch a few rides in. She was totally stoked. As she got beyond the break, Aileana turned around toward the beach and watched the first set. She found some small swells and decided to take off. Aileana popped up to her goofy-footed stance. Then angling to the right, took a smooth ride until she kicked-out and headed back out beyond the break again. She kept at the waves for another hour or so. The whole time she'd been surfing, she noticed she'd acquired an inquisitive group of watchers, of the sea mammal variety.

The waves were pretty small today so she decided to paddle over to the pillars and just veg-out for a while. She paddled out near the pillars and Aileana saw it was quite the happening hangout, for the seals. The local seals were out in force. Seal-wise it was busier than *The 405* during rush hour.

Aileana was as close to the rocks as she could get without getting smashed into them by the wave action.

The seals were watching her with interest. And she enjoyed watching them darting back and forth among the base of the pillars. Some of the seals seemed like they were playing tag or some game they had made up with each other. The gray seals off the coast of Scotland seemed to be somewhat larger than the California sea lions, which she saw in Malibu all the time.

Aileana decided to paddle around the interesting rock formation to check it out. As she paddled around, she noticed one large handsome fellow. This seal watched her with an intensity which was slightly spooky. He looked a little different from most of the grays out there. He was a lot larger than the rest and his head was not the same shape of a gray. His snout wasn't as hooked as a gray. His eyes were so beautiful and more expressive than the other seals. His fur was also a dark blackish-brown instead of the dapple coloring of the grays. It was strange, but she could almost swear he was following her in the water as she paddled around the rocks. Possibly he thought she was a strange form of seal, because of her black wetsuit.

She started to talk to him. "Hey, boy, whatcha doing following me out here? Do you want to learn to surf? I betcha you would be a natural." She laughed at herself talking to the seal. "What shall I call you? I assume you're a dude, so I am going to call you Mr. Seal," she said to him. He must have liked the name because he decided to swim a little closer. She backed up because her father had always told her and her sister not to touch the sea creatures. "You don't want the sea creatures to get a false sense of security;

they may approach the wrong person. They might get the impression all people are good and won't hurt them."

Mr. Seal was persistent and kept coming closer and closer and even started to rest his head on the front of the board, looking Aileana right in the eye.

"What a strange friendly fellow you are. Why aren't you playing with the other seals instead of hanging with me? You know I'm not a seal, don't ya?" He gave a bark as if he was answering. "Well, I guess we can be surfing buddies then. I'm done for the day and should go back to shore. I need to get some work done, to try and earn my living." He slid off the end of the board as if he understood what Aileana had said. As he left, she felt him swim up against her hand that was in the water getting ready to paddle back to shore. His pelt was soft and silky in texture, but Aileana could feel the animal's solid, hard muscles just below his skin. He was a large, powerful creature and so utterly beautiful, with such graceful movements. His touch gave her a strange sensation at the time he brushed against her. There was some sort of undercurrent surging through his body.

As she paddled back to shore, she kept thinking about the friendly seal. She wondered why she sensed a strange connection to the large dark seal, and what was that surge of energy that had passed from him to her? The seals back home were outgoing, but not that approachable. Evidently, Scottish seals were a lot friendlier.

She walked into *Seanmhair's* cottage to the most wonderful aroma coming from the kitchen. The fragrant scent of butter and sugar caramelizing made her mouth water. She couldn't wait to sample the rich, crumbly and sugary delight that literally melted in your mouth. Her *seanmhair* had finished up a batch of her famous Scottish Tablet. The scent took her right back to her childhood summers spent here, wrapped in a warm cocoon of love.

"Yer in time to try this batch of candy; I'm taking a plate of it over to my friend Angus. He has been feeling poorly and I thought it may cheer him up," Skye said as she prepared the plate.

"Angus, isn't he the man who owns the little grocery store in the village?"

"Aye, that's Angus, and there's not a nicer man around. He's having a wee bit of back problems. He should be better soon. I think my Scottish Tablet weel help him with his troubles." She laughed.

"Is that so, *Seanmhair*? I didn't know there were magical powers in your candy?"

"The only magic in the candy is showing friends ye care, *mo nighean*."

"*Seanmhair*, I was out in the water today, catching a few waves. Then I relaxed on my shortboard near the pillars. Out beyond the breakwater, I came across an immense dark seal. Have you heard anything about the seals being extremely friendly?"

"Nay, people in the village haven't mentioned anything about the seals. Perhaps a Selkie was being friendly with ye, Aileana." She laughed. "If 'twas a Selkie, it is believed they bring luck to the ones they choose to befriend."

"*Seanmhair*, you and your tales of Selkies, just like when I was a child. But I could use some of the luck you're talking about, considering my last disastrous choice in boyfriends, and my deadline for the article I'm writing for the magazine. Some luck would be appreciated about now." She chuckled at the thought.

Chapter 5

Kendrick

Kendrick was relieved to find himself alone in this area of the drilling platform above the calm sea on such a *brèagha* early morning as the sun started to rise above the horizon and the morning mist. This was the first time he had any peace since his shift on the rig started two days ago. Most of the men were still in their bunks, and only a small night crew was at work, which kept the rig running smoothly. Soon, the day crew would be up and in the mess hall, getting their breakfast before starting their work shift.

The majority of the men on the rig were hardworking family men trying to make an honest living. So far, he'd only run into a couple of men who were not as honest as they wanted everyone to believe. There were, in fact, only two men who were corrupt and up to something. He just wasn't sure what they were hiding, but he was close to finding out.

This jack-up unit out-produced some of the other rigs in the Northern Sea, which made this oil platform extremely valuable to the oil company. The company ran a tight operation and had a good safety record. The men on this mobile offshore drilling unit were also treated well by the company. The company knew that the happier the men were the harder they worked.

As far as he could tell, the men that now worked on the oil rig were not like the men that had killed his brother. Kendrick thanked the powers that be, the Scottish Marine Act passed in 2010 that made it an offense to shoot seals in Scotland.

He heard that the salmon fishermen around Murkle/Dunnet Bay about a mile from Thurso, armed with rifles to kill a large population of seals they felt were stealing their salmon profits. Fortunately, volunteers from the marine conservation society, *Sea Shepherd UK*, arrived with two boats to defend the seals. The activists planned to stop any killing of the seals; they were also patrolling for any illegal fishing in the area. The *Sea Shepherd*, he was sure had not only saved the area seals, but also some of his Selkie Clan.

He had heard the two men who had killed his brother Callum, had died soon after they had signed on with a fishing boat. The authorities had ruled it an accident, saying they had drowned after they got tangled and pulled down in their fishing nets. Even Kendrick wasn't sure if their death had actually been an accident or payback from his brother's Selkie friends. It was well known that Selkies would avenge their kindred if they were wronged or harmed.

Even after finding out the men who killed his brother were dead, it did not heal his grief-stricken heart. His brother and he were close, closer than a lot of brothers. They had shared a dream of making a difference for their Selkie Clan. Now that he was gone, Kendrick needed to make sure the clan came first.

His brother Callum had spent most of his time learning how to be the future ruler by spending his days with their *athair*, their father. But Callum always had time for his two younger brothers. They had regularly swum together to visit with other Selkie clans around Scotland and Ireland. They wanted to understand what concerns the other clans had. They were their father's eyes and ears to make sure the clans were happy.

His younger brother Duncan had thought about getting a job on the oil rig. Duncan wanted to work with Kendrick and some his own friends from the village. This would be Duncan's chance to get to know what was going on the topside of the rig. Duncan was a bit of a wild man who actually didn't want to settle down in any way shape or form. His thoughts and feeling on settling down were, "Why do that? Why settle when the ocean and land are my oyster, so to speak?" He was altogether delighted to make all the ladies happy, not just one. He used his Selkie magic to get what he wanted, and it never failed him. Up until recently, he was all too happy to only take odd jobs here and there. Now, for some reason, Duncan focused on an oil rig job. Moreover, it was a move in the right direction where his family was concerned.

Duncan also realized he needed to spend some time with Kendrick. He needed to start learning how to be his brother's second-in-command as Kendrick would now be the Lord of the Selkies when their father stepped down. Their family felt he should start learning the family business of ruling the Selkies. Duncan didn't feel learning the family business should get too much in the way of his pleasure with the females of either species. Besides, it would come down to Kendrick being the ruler of the Selkies.

The quiet of the early morning faded fast as the sun was on the rise in the eastern horizon. The voices of the men who were up and about carried over the platform. It was time Kendrick, too, started his job. He needed to stop his thoughts of Aileana Sutherland, whom he fished out of the sea four nights past.

He also had a chance to see Aileana out surfing and sunning on her board the next day after the storm. Kendrick had been surprised to see her back in the water after almost drowning. Little did she know he was the seal she named "Mr. Seal." This opportunity gave him a chance to watch her without her realizing it was him. She was just as he remembered her from that summer twelve years ago. She was a self-confident woman now, still headstrong and fearless. Aileana, he believed, fit her Clan Sutherland's motto to a T. Their clan motto was *San Peur* which meant "Without Fear." She also seemed to be without guile, but she had no way to know it was Kendrick in his Selkie form and not a seal. He found it hard in so many ways to stop his thoughts from going back to her tight body and plump pink lips. Aileana's lips were so desirable, they begged him to taste their lushness.

During his work shift of twenty-eight days, he had plenty of backbreaking work to keep her out of his mind. But keeping his mind occupied during his time working on the jack-up rig wasn't the problem. With twelve long hours each shift, it was the off work time in his bunk which were the ones he wasn't dealing with so well. But nevertheless, when his current working shift ended, he would have the next twenty-eight days free. He would most likely cross her path in the village. He thought he didn't have time in his life for the complication of a female, even one so enticing.

He needed to think about getting on his new Harley Street Glide Special to take his mind off the complication of that particular female. Riding his bike always did the trick in the past, to make him forget problems and difficulties in his life. What he needed was some uncomplicated sex. He needed something that would ease the tightness in the front of his pants. Only three days had passed, it would be a long twenty-five days until he could do something about the pressing issue of his cock, besides the use of his hand.

Chapter 6

Finman

The Finman was out in the water, close to shore hunting for his prey. He spotted the lone female walking along the beach. His dark eyes searched the shore to see if she was with another human. It seemed she was out here on her own. The evil sorcerous shapeshifter floated to shore as a harmless piece of seaweed. Seaweed was something no one would think twice about. As the Finman floated to shore, he waited until the female walked past the seaweed. He rose up to stand in his humanoid form. At seven feet tall, he was gauntly built and had a dark countenance on his harsh face.

Without the human aware he was behind her, he grabbed her from behind. She shrieked like a banshee and thrashed her arms and legs. The Finman used his fist to shut the howling human up. He had to be careful, humans were so fragile. He threw her over his slumped shoulder and started to turn her way to the beach. He moved back into the water with his victim over his bony shoulder. The blonde female he held was now quiet and hung limp after he had shut up her wailing. toward the sea. It was then he heard another human yell at him.

The Finman glanced up at the cliffs above and spotted the human female. It was the same one the Selkie had stolen from him a few days ago. Now he knew where to find the redheaded human bitch. He would make that Selkie pay for interfering with his planned abduction.

He needed to blend back into the sea before the female on the cliff made

He would use this female for his needs till he was able to steal the fiery redhead. She was the one he wanted to beget his heirs with, he would use his evil magic to change her mind. He would consider it restitution for the trouble the damn Selkie caused him. She appeared to be on the small side, perhaps her feisty spirit would make up for her puny size. The shape-shifter could feel his cock stiffen at the thought of the redheaded bitch. For now, he would put this human on his shoulder to work once he returned to the hidden island of Hildaland.

This blonde human should work out well to meet his needs. Then, if she was still alive when he kidnapped the fiery redhead, he would sell the blonde and make a tidy profit. He smirked as he thought of the silver this blonde would bring. She would be well used and submissive by the time he sold her to his clan. She was a sturdy human that should be able to tolerate being a wife of one of the Finman. The evil Finman laughed to himself at the thought of what his clan would pay for such a beauty.

Chapter 7

Aileana

Aileana sat at the desk by the window, trying to put some time in on her article she was writing for the magazine. But she wasn't having much luck with the information from the locals. They all had too much to lose if it got out they talked to a journalist about the oil rigs. Aileana felt like she was butting her head against a stone wall. Someone had to be willing to talk; she just needed to find a person who would.

She decided to catch up with her emails and write a few quick messages to her parents and her sister. Aileana planned to Skype with them later in the week at a time she knew would be convenient for them.

She was in the process of deleting a bunch of junk email from her account when she heard a faint, terrified scream from down below on the beach. Aileana jumped up from the computer and grabbed the binoculars her seanmhair left lying on the ledge of the large window facing the ocean. Near the rocks along the shore, a gigantic man was carrying a struggling woman over his shoulder toward the water.

She ran out the door as fast as her legs would carry her. She cupped her hands around her mouth and shouted down to the gargantuan-sized man. "What in the hell do you think you're doing? Leave her alone, you shithole."

Aileana definitely was not thinking clearly. She had nothing on her person to try and help the woman. Where was her mace spray when she needed it?

She heard screams for help; the woman put up a good fight from the sounds that came from the beach. Aileana planned to jump on the brute to help the woman as soon as she reached them. Aileana was small and petite, but she could be vicious if needed. She was ready to use her nails and teeth if it came to that.

Aileana took the steep stairway down with its twists and turns all the way to the beach. She'd lost sight of the two of them struggling and now couldn't hear any cries for help. What the hell? It hadn't taken her more than a few minutes to reach the beach. Where were they? They'd both just disappeared into thin air. She ran to the area where she last saw them, but only saw a set of deep footprints being washed away by the waves and rising tide.

Aileana rushed back to the cottage after finding no trace of either the man or the woman on the beach. She placed a call to the local police station to report what she'd seen. They told her they would send a man out to take a report.

Half an hour later an officer knocked on the door of the cottage. Since her grandmother was still in town doing some shopping, she answered the door to find a uniformed officer. He introduced himself as Officer Sinclair. The officer had bright red hair and freckles covered his face. Officer Sinclair seemed to be about thirty years old. He was a short, stocky man with a serious no-nonsense attitude. Aileana showed him in and started to give him the details of what she had seen.

"I was sitting at my laptop going over some of my emails when I heard the screams," she told him.

"Could ye make out any words that were being spoken? Perhaps it was a lovers' tiff?"

"That was no lovers' quarrel that I've ever seen or heard, she sounded like she was fighting for her life and screaming at the top of her lungs," she hotly replied.

"And what did this assailant look like? Did ye get a clear view?" He continued writing down everything she said.

"Well, he was gaunt, gigantic, really incredibly tall, around seven feet tall. His build was slight. He must have weighed around a hundred and eighty pounds. I'm not sure what the pounds versus stones conversion are. He looked enormous, and had wet shoulder length, dark brown hair."

"How were ye able to see a clear view of him from this distance?" the officer asked.

"I used my grandmother's binoculars." She pointed to the pair now lying on the couch, where she had thrown them when she ran out the door.

"Could ye make out what he was wearing?"

"Just, in general, it appeared he had some seaweed wrapped around his shorts or bathing suit, or maybe it was caught on them. It was hard to tell from this distance, even with the binoculars. He wasn't wearing a shirt. He was pale-skinned, almost albino white and long-limbed."

"What did ye observe when ye reached the beach?"

"That is the strange part. I couldn't see or hear the woman or the man at all. No trace of them except for some large footprints that were rather deep. But the footprints were starting to wash away with the tide by the time I was in the spot that I had seen them. How could two people just vanish like that?"

"Did ye notice if they might be out in the water?"

"I scanned the surf and beyond, I couldn't see anyone on the beach. The water had no one in it that I could see. Not even the seals that are usually out beyond the surf," she stated.

All right, I guess that is it. I will turn the report in at the station. We will check for a missing woman in the area and go from there. Yer description isn't too clear other than a large-sized male. Ye were quite a ways away, I understand. We will put up some bulletins around town to see if anyone has seen someone that size around," he said. "Ye will be around if we have any other questions?"

"Of course, please let me know if you find the woman. It would ease my mind to know she is okay. And it was just some loud lovers' quarrel." She didn't believe that was going to be the case.

Chapter 8

Kendrick

He received a message from his father that his brother Duncan would arrive in Durness to help with a Finfolk problem. Lord Murdock had sent a communication to the local Selkies of Durness. He stated the Finfolk had been sighted in the area and rumored to be looking for humans to make their spouses or slaves.

The Finfolk were dangerous sea creatures who preyed on humans; male and female alike. They were the malevolent cousins to the Selkies. They were highly aggressive when they felt a fisherman or anyone else has entered their perceived territory.

It had been said that female Finfolk started their life as beautiful mermaids. They always would prefer to have a human as a husband. If the mermaid took a Finman to be her husband, they were doomed to become a hideously revolting Finwife. They got uglier each year as they aged until they were a hag. Also, a marriage to a male Finfolk was most always unhappy as they were cruel and beat their wives and slaves.

They had aggressive tactics when it comes to acquiring a spouse. The women used trickery to seduce unsuspecting human males. The male Finfolk hunted down human women and spirited them away from their family, never to be seen again.

The Finfolk were greedy creatures and could disguise themselves as other sea animals, plants, or even floating clothes so that they could leap upon unsuspecting humans and seize them to use as spouses or slaves. The Finfolk have but one weakness, for silver coins and silver objects.

Kendrick needed his brother and at least another Selkie friend to watch the shoreline and the coast in the area around Durness in case some of the local villagers should turn up missing. He contacted Duncan and his friend Torin. They were due to arrive within the next two or three days. They would set up a patrol offshore and watch for the Finfolk. This was the time of year that Finfolk liked to waylay unsuspecting fishermen or women out on the beaches.

Kendrick met up with Duncan and Torin on the second day after contacting them. He explained the situation to both his friend and brother, about the sighting of the Unseelie Finfolk. They decided to have two patrolling in the water at night and the other on the beach patrolling. They decided to guard the beach and water area closest to the town as that would be the area Finfolk would choose.

Duncan asked, "So, brother, besides those shape-shifting sorcerers, what else has kept ye in Durness this past week? Customarily on yer time off the rig, ye would make a trip to see our parents."

"Brother, I have seen someone from mah past, a human female. I need to find out why I can't get her off mah mind. It is most likely only because I remember her when she was but a wean." he replied.

"Don't forget who yer talking to, Kendrick. I know what ye want to know and how ye want to know her." He laughed

"Just because ye can't keep it in yer pants around females doesn't mean that is how it is for me with Aileana."

"Oh, so her name is Aileana," Duncan said.

"Aye, Aileana Sutherland. I am sure she is here staying at Skye Sutherland's cottage. Skye is her *seanmhair*."

"Weel, perhaps I should go and introduce myself to this Aileana who has ye so intrigued. She should have a chance to meet, the better-looking brother," Duncan replied.

"I am sure ye'll have a chance to meet her, but she is mine till I figure what is between us."

"Okay, okay, big brother, I won't get in yer way, till ye say ye don't want her. Then, I will be glad to take her off yer hands." He smiled.

"Now if ye two sea cocks are finished with yer pissing contest, we need to work out a plan to keep the humans in the village safe from the Finfolk." Torin looked from one brother to the next.

He nodded toward Torin and Duncan and stated, "There is talk in the village of a young woman missing. There are also some bulletins posted regarding a huge man seen carrying a young woman away. Sounds as if the Finmen are already here and taking unwilling brides."

"I am sure the woman will not be seen again. She will already be on their hidden island of Hildaland," Duncan replied.

"Aye, and we won't be able to find the Hildaland because of that damn magical fog which surrounds the island. We kin only find a bonded life mate if they're taken. That bond is our only hope with our females," Kendrick stated.

Chapter 9

Aileana

She felt right at home, living in her *seanmhair's* cottage and with Scotland as her new address. Scotland had actually always been her second home. It was going to take only a small amount of time to get acclimated to her new living arrangement and the Scots' way of life.

Aileana decided she should take a walk into town to see if any of her friends might be out and about. It was a magnificent sunny day, now that the morning mist had burned off. As she walked along the sidewalk in town, the smell of the ocean and green hills made her feel so wonderful and content. She could genuinely appreciate the splendor of the country here, she loved that she was able to see the rolling hills and rocky creags. It was so different from the San Fernando Valley, where she had always called home. The valley was wholly housing tracts and asphalt streets. Where one town left off, another started. There were no open spaces anymore unless one counted the small pocket parks that were an afterthought in the city planning. At least in northern Scotland, she felt her heart could mend from the betrayal she'd suffered.

Up the street, she could see the local pub. She was hungry; she hadn't eaten that morning. Aileana walked into the lively pub. There she was, surrounded by loud laughing men filling the pub. The pub had a rich dark aroma of flowing beer. She was aware there was to be a shift change out on the oil rig. The pub sure appeared as if it had already taken place. The animated tavern was nearly filled with what she thought were the single guys. Aileana hoped all the married men would be home enjoying their off time with their wives and family.

The testosterone level was quite high in the pub as the men were all bragging about one thing or another. She could hear a group of rowdy men laughing about some off-color story one of the oil riggers was revealing. The room had a friendly vibe, lots of beer drinking and cheerful men.

She walked over to the bar to place her order for the sampler platter of shrimp, scallops, and mussels in white wine, butter, and garlic broth. The platter was served with a chunk of warm, dark Scottish oat bread with a generous portion of soft creamy butter. She decided to go with a white wine since her seafood platter came in a wine broth.

She thought it was a good thing she had been getting her walks in the morning and surfing an hour or so in the afternoons. Or else she wouldn't be able to get through the pub doors. Just as she got ready to take a seat toward the back of the pub so she could watch all the local action. She noticed one of the men who was the size of a mountain and as solid as a block wall, who played a mean game of darts with his cohorts and seemed to fill the tavern. Dart Man backed-up and bumped her glass of Sauvignon Blanc, which splashed down the front of her green plaid woolen Pendleton shirt. The big beast of a man had been laughing with his buddies and was unaware she walked behind him. He spun around and started to apologize when his mouth quirked into a wicked smile.

She sputtered. "What's so funny, dude?"

"Nothing is funny, I just smiled because I ken ye!"

Aileana took a closer look at him after she started to wipe the Sauvignon off her chest.

"Oh my God, Kendrick, is that you? You look exactly the same as you did when we first met. Damn, you've got some good genes, and I am not talking the jeans you have on." She laughed.

"Thanks." He laughed. "It runs in our family, lucky I guess. Aileana, yer a wonderful sight to behold, ye'v grown up to be a bonnie lass."

"Thank you; it's been a long time. What are you up to now?"

"I finished mah twenty-eight-day shift on the oil rig. Decided to come into town and blow off some steam with mah friends. Are ye staying with yer *seanmhair* for a visit?"

"Yes, I am at her cottage for the time being. I am here for more than a visit, though, I plan on staying at least a year if not more. I only need a computer and an internet connection to do my job."

"What type of work are ye doing?"

"I work for a magazine that does various types of news stories. In fact, the piece I am working on now is about offshore oil rigs in Scotland. Maybe I can pick your brain and get various inside information," she replied.

"Sure, although I'm nae certain what I kin tell ye, I'm simply a roustabout."

"Excellent! You just never know what information I will find useful."

"Why don't ye let me buy ye another glass of wine, and we kin catch up some."

"That sounds wonderful, I would love to catch up, and you can help me finish my seafood platter. I'm sure my eyes are bigger than my stomach."

"Now, that is a temptation I won't say nay to ye. Mah favorite food is shellfish." He laughed.

"I took you for a steak and potatoes man."

"Aye, I enjoy them also, but shellfish and any seafood are mah favorites. So what have ye been up to, lass? Are ye breaking all the men's hearts back home?" He grinned.

"After high school, I went to the University of Southern California and got my degree in Journalism. Now, I earn my living working for *All News Magazine*. I love my job because I enjoy the freedom to go where I want, and write about anything that is newsworthy."

"What brought ye to Scotland to stay a year or so, lass?"

"Well, I needed a change of scenery. I had a nasty break up with a lying, cheating dirt bag of a boyfriend," she replied with a grimace.

"Weel, ye sure don't sugarcoat yer feelings toward this man. Do ye need me to pound him to dust for ye, lass?"

"No, the dipshit is not worth the effort, but thanks for the offer." She smiled back at his grinning face. "What are you doing besides working on the oil rigs? How is your family?"

"Besides the work on the rig, I also help mah *athair*, my father, learning the family business, basically to serve our clan. Mah family is doing all right, except for the loss of our oldest brother."

"Kendrick, I am so sorry. I can't imagine the loss of a sibling. My heart goes out to you and your family; I have no words to express what it must be like to lose someone so close."

"It's been five years now, and yet it feels like only yesterday. Callum and I were tight; I lost mah brother who also happened to be mah best friend. We're a close-knit family, but brothers always have a tighter bond. I am sure ye share the same attachment with yer sister. What was her name?"

"Adaira."

Chapter 10

Kendrick

After he literally bumped into Aileana at the pub yesterday, they decided to go on a hike the next morning to the local moors. Kendrick met up with her in front of the local Bed and Breakfast in town.

She was decked out like she knew what a Scottish hike was, down to the prerequisite day pack. Aileana wore faded blue Levi's and dark blue thermal shirt with a red plaid flannel shirt, along with her hiking boots. She had a black baseball cap pulled down low on her head. Her dark auburn hair pulled back in a low ponytail, the long, loose waves hung to her narrow waist. The Wayfarer sunglasses were hiding her large, luminous dark green eyes.

There was something that was so attractive about a woman who didn't have to be wearing a fancy dress and all that war paint on her face. Aileana was a natural beauty, a woman who was at home in her own skin. Her attitude appeared to be, 'this is me, deal with it or not, I like myself, hope you do too'. The same attitude she had as a confident teenager.

She also relished her tomboy ways, but she seemed to enjoy being all female when she wished. It was almost as if she loved to keep people off balance and guessing when it came to knowing who the real Aileana was.

She saw Kendrick then.

"Good morning, hope ye slept well and are rested. I thought we would hike over toward Loch Croispol today. I brought a few pieces of fruit and bottled water in mah backpack," he said to her. He watched her smile; it lit up her lovely face.

"Good. That should go well with the brownies I made. I also brought cheese and salami, along with a couple slices of my *seanmhair's* brown bread. It sounds like we're not going hungry today." She laughed. "So we're headed to the area around Loch Croispol. Sounds like an ideal hike."

'It's a *brèagha* hike this time of year, ye will enjoy it."

She grinned as she said, "Let's hit the road, Jack, or the trails, whatever."

After about two hours of hiking and showing her the Scottish countryside, they decided to take a breather. They had taken the small least used trails, which were slow going, but the most scenic. They crested a small sized mountain and both agreed that this was a perfect place to stop.

"This countryside is magnificent; it always takes my breath away. I've not hiked here in years." She sighed. "It's been way too long."

"I just can't believe that ye're, here again. I had wondered if ye were still coming to Scotland each year. I didnae approach yer *seanmhair* to ask as I thought it would seem strange for a grown male to be asking after a teenage lass."

She laughed as she said, "I'm so sure, *Seanmhair* would have wondered if you might be some kind of perv. Even though you were always a gentleman in our friendship. Now that I am grown, she wouldn't bat an eye at you asking. I often wondered what you were doing each summer I came to visit my *seanmhair*."

"I mainly helped my athair in the family business or worked on the oil rig. I see ye still have the pink pearl. It looks lovely made into a necklace; I was surprised to see ye wearing it at the pub when I bumped into ye."

"Yes, the pearl, I had it made up that fall after I got back home to the States. Because of the teardrop shape, I decided to add three small diamonds in an inverted triangle at the top to show off the beauty and the unusual shape of the pearl."

"The pearl does your beauty, justice," he said with a wink and a nod to her.

"Did you go to Ireland and kiss the Blarney Stone?"

"Nay, lass, I only speak the truth, when I talk with ye. Ye have ken I am honest with ye."

"What a refreshing idea from a male!"

"Ouch! Sounds as if ye'v had a problem or two, with the male species."

"That is part of the reason I decided to come to Scotland to stay. Not that I ran away, but I wanted a fresh start," she said.

"Nay, I would never think yer the type of woman to run!"

"My philosophy is when one door closes, another opens," she stated as she laid back and started viewing the clouds above.

Kendrick tried to watch her without looking too obvious. She had a contented smile on her lips. He desperately wanted to sample her lush pink lips so, he decided to take a chance and damn the consequences. He needed to know if his desires were one-sided or hopefully would be reciprocated.

She turned her head. "Why are you watching so intensely?"

"Well, that's what males do. When we see something we want."

She laughed. "You want me? Why don't you let me sample one of your kisses to see if I want you?"

Her brazen response was all the encouragement Kendrick needed. His erection strained and pushed against his fly. He moved closer to her, trying to make adjustments in his jeans, without her seeing that his body reacted to her like an inexperienced youth.

He zeroed in on those full pink lips like a dive bomber going in for the kill. He slid his lips across her lush mouth, savoring the feel and taste of her soft sweet lips. He was in sensory overload, tasting and feeling, and her skin smelled of honey and spice. Kendrick's brain was in a fog as he tried to process the smell of her skin and the sweet nectar of her lips. He sensed there was more to his feelings than just appreciating Aileana's body.

Kendrick had to have more. He started to sip at her lips and glided his tongue along the seam of her mouth until he felt her lips start to open to his. He plunged his tongue inside. Her tongue sparred with his, stroke for stroke. This was no timid lass, but a hot-blooded woman, who could give as well as she received.

"Lass, yer taste outshines the finest wine." he murmured. Then he brought his lips to her slender neck. His tongue swirled up her neck, and it slid up to her small seashell shaped ear. He ran the tip of his tongue along the edge of her ear and dipped into the shell. He heard her soft moans as he gently probed her. He ran his fingers through the long length of her silky auburn hair. He moved his hands to cup her face as he then went back to her mouth to taste her sweet nectar. He felt as if he'd been drugged and was now an addict for her sweetness.

Kendrick hands slowly slid down her neck to her shoulders, holding and caressing her. His right hand moved to the swell of her breast, to cup a young, firm, lush handful.

His thumb stroked her nipple to an erect peak. He could feel her heart as it started beating wildly beneath her breast. The Selkie in him could smell the sweet spice of her arousal. He knew she would be wet between her legs. His erection was now painful, enormous and hard like a field cannon.

He brought his lips to her nipple and sucked, taking each in turn through her thermal shirt. The swollen pebbled peaks were too enticing to resist. They wanted his attention and wanted to be free to feel his rough tongue and be licked to even harder peaks. He wanted to taste her sweet flesh and bite those sweet peaks until she screamed his name in bliss.

As their passion took them higher, he pulled her on top of him as he rolled onto his back. Kendrick wanted her to feel what he wanted to plant deep in her body. He was able to make small sliding motions with her body against his. His cock was at the juncture of her mons. He hadn't dry humped with a lass since he was an untried young lad. The gentle stroking of their bodies made all the sensations more intense as he slid her against himself. He knew he was close to making a wet mess in his pants and that wasn't going to happen.

He reached for her hand and placed it on his erection. She pressed against his rigid length and gripped him with his Levi's between her hand and his dick. He started to move his hand to unbutton his fly. He was ready to rip the buttons open, but she stopped his hand with her own. He groaned as he became aware she put the brakes on their building lust.

"I'm not ready to take this any further than what we're doing now. I know that sounds somewhat out of place considering I have my hand glued to the front of your pants. I can't think clearly and I am not ready to jump into this. Please try to understand." Her voice was husky with unspent passion.

"*Bheag aon,* little one, I am not going to rush ye now or ever. Dinna fash I understand that someone hurt ye before. We will move at whatever pace ye need. Ye just turn my world inside out when I am with ye," he whispered.

It was agony to let her go and not fill her with his aching thick length. But he realized that if he wanted her as his sweet prize, he had to stop and let her set the pace. In the end, he hoped he would be the one to reap the rewards for his patience. She was more than just a conquest. He wasn't sure what it was, but he kept feeling there was something more important than just a quick release.

After he liberated her from his arms and mouth, Kendrick sat up slowly in an effort to get his bearings back. He attempted to make their banter light and easy between them. He didn't want to let her go, but he didn't want her to run from his touch. He could have used his Selkie magic to get what he wanted, but that was not how he wanted her to come to him. He wanted her, on her own, to need him as much as he felt the need for her.

With any other human woman, he would use his magic to seduce them to make them want him. But for some reason, his conscience would not let him use his magic on her. With Aileana, he didn't want to use the magic he wanted her to choose him. Was it that he still remembered her as trusting young lass? Who he knew then as a friend or was it some other reason his mind still hadn't made clear to him?

He said to her, "Let's have some nourishment for our walk back home. Let me try some of yer homemade brownies. I want to see what kind of cook ye are." He winked at her and smiled playfully to lighten the mood.

"I will have you know I'm a fantastic cook, and making brownies is baking, not cooking." She laughed.

"Well, as ye say, whatever! Let's try them out and see if ye're a respectable baker or not!"

After they finished their packed lunch, they started their hike back to the village. Aileana took the time to snap pictures of the countryside and various flowers. They talked briefly to a couple of sheep crofters that they came across on the way back home. She had various questions about the new lambs in the flock of sheep. She was such a curious woman always wanting more knowledge, perhaps that was the writer in her. The sun started to set as they reached her *seanmhair's* cottage door.

"Aileana, I enjoyed our day together and want to enjoy more of them with ye,"

"I enjoyed being with you. It was a wonderful day filled with pleasant surprises! I loved hearing about what you have been doing, the last twelve years. You're easy to talk to and be with."

"So ye're okay with the surprises! I didnae mean to frighten ye off," he said.

"Hell no, it takes a lot more to scare me off. I do like surprises when I am in the right frame of mind. I'm just not on the same page as you are yet." She smiled.

So taking a cue from her words, he leaned down to take her in his arms. He pulled her close to his body, enjoying the feel her lithe body as it started to mold to his. He took his hand and pulled her head to his and nibbled on her lower lip until he felt her lips open to his. He dipped his tongue in to taste her sweet mouth.

He took his time with that one kiss and then stepped back and let her go. The look on her face said it all. It had the desired effect; he wanted to leave her wanting more. God help him because leaving was one of the toughest things he'd ever done. His body protested in a big, hard and uncomfortable way not to leave. He guessed it was time this Selkie took a long swim and tried to work off some of that lust and frustration.

Chapter 11

Aileana

She sat at the table by the window which overlooked the sea, busy writing her story about the offshore oil drilling in the area. Preparing the article to be sent to the magazine editor.

When she glanced up, Kendrick stood there, leaning against the door frame. He was such a large man he seemed to fill the cottage and leave little space for anything else.

"Hello, hope I didn't startle ye. Yer *seanmhair's* friend let me in the cottage. She said Skye was busy in the kitchen and ye were in the living room working," Kendrick said.

"I've been so occupied I didn't even know *Seanmhair* had a friend visiting. Did you come to tell me you will sell me the story on the oil rigs? The magazine will pay you for the inside information on what they're doing out there."

Kendrick regarded her. "I've my own reasons for being on the rig, and I don't need your employer's money. Maybe someday I will share my reason with ye, but not yer magazine." Kendrick then gazed out at the sea as he said, "Ye will just have to trust me on this."

"I trust you, but it would be easier if I understood the whole story."

Aileana thought about her *seanmhair* being so upset about the oil rigs in the local area. Could the two be related in some way? Why the hell did her *seanmhair* care about the offshore oil rigs?

"You know, I believe *Seanmhair's* concerned about the impact the rigs will have on the area, what do you think about that?"

Kendrick walked over to the large brown worn wingback chair by the fireplace, where he sat down and stretched his long, well-muscled legs.

"Yer grandmother's a kind and loving woman. It's not a surprise she'd have an interest in the ocean and all creatures in it, she lives next to the sea. It's only natural she doesn't want the oil platforms in the area offshore. There's is always a chance of oil spills would destroy the ocean's ecosystem for miles around. Fish and other sea animals would be killed or suffer from the effects of an oil spill. Money is nae the answer to all problems," he said.

"She mentions the 'Selkie' folk tales as if they are real. And not disturbing the sea floor is more important than the jobs and money that the oil rigs will bring to this town. I don't understand her belief in magical sea creatures. I could better understand her worrying about the possibility of an oil spill. I don't want any more, platforms built as they do affect the life of the seals, porpoises and the minke whales off the coast."

"It does affect all the sea creatures more than ye can imagine." There was a sad note in his voice.

"That's why I'm writing this article for the magazine, to see if we can get them to stop building any more rigs in the area. One is more than enough."

"The main reason I dropped over was to see if ye would like to get together tomorrow evening. I thought ye might enjoy going out after working so hard on yer article. That way ye will have time to work during the day and we will get together in the evening."

"That sound great, it's a date then."

Chapter 12

Aileana

She spied the seal as he climbed out of the water and onto the rocks. He looked to be her Mr. Seal. He was out beyond the breakers on one of the quartzite pillars which the local seals used to bask in the sun.

The seal seemed to shed his skin of silky black fur. The shape before her was not his true shape. Unexpectedly, there on the rocks stood a large, naked, and powerful man. Had she now completely lost her mind, or could the local legends of the seals being Selkies be true?

As Aileana watched this seal man, he dove into the water and headed to the beach. She tried to remember the tales her *seanmhair* had so often told her as a child, about the Selkies of Scotland. Her *seanmhair* had told Aileana the Selkies had their own magic. And Selkies had lived in the northern Scottish seas long before the Vikings had even come to this area of the world.

Her *seanmhair* had told stories of Selkies who would take a local lass for their lover. She told her, "Guard your heart, for heartache comes to young lassies who fall in love with Selkie men." She also told her the Selkies were known to leave their lovers and return to their home, the sea. The most fortunate of the women were the ones the Selkies choose for their life mates. Because no human could even hope to compare to having a Selkie lover. Aileana remembered asking her *seanmhair* what she meant by that statement? But her grandmother had simply laughed and said, "Now, there's a tale to be told when you're older."

Seanmhair also told Aileana she once knew a Selkie when she was a young woman. Aileana was only a child and had paid little attention to these stories when her *seanmhair* told the local folk tales. She had believed they were only fairy tales, such as her favorite, *Beauty and the Beast*. Now she wished she had paid more heed to those tales told to her long ago.

She hid behind a large rock up near the cave because she didn't want to be seen by the man or seal man, or whatever he was. As he walked closer, she saw it was Kendrick in all his naked glory, and this wasn't Black's Beach either. His rock-hard, virile body was built like Aileana's version of Poseidon the God of the Sea from what she could see at this distance. Her gaze followed the lines of Kendrick's well-developed shoulders to his bulging biceps, and down to his hard abs. She peered further down to a deep V below his belly button where the solid ridge of his abs ended. There, his thick and incredibly long shaft rested on his heavy sac. She knew he was large, but holy mother of Eros!

After she gathered her wicked thoughts together, Aileana's mind came back to the fact of what she had just seen, besides him having a magnificent body. The man she was starting to have feelings for wasn't a man, but a Selkie! She had feelings for a Selkie! What a mess she was in, and what would she do with this knowledge? Who should she talk to, her grandmother or Kendrick? She needed answers now and not later. Aileana decided she would go and talk to Kendrick first. She needed her answers to come from the not-so-mythical source. The journalist in her needed the true story, even if it was for her ears only.

Aileana waited by the boulder until she saw him walk out of the small sea cave now dressed in his swim trunks. She tried to gather her thoughts and come up with coherent sentences to ask Kendrick the necessary questions. Considering the issue, that would be a rather tricky deal. Would Kendrick even admit what she had seen was real?

Lana Lea Short

Would he be honest with her, or would he try to play it off that she was delusional? She needed the truth and not some child's fable. Her mind would not rest until she had all the information about the nature of this sea creature or Selkie man.

Chapter 13

Kendrick

After a strenuous morning swim in his Selkie form, he enjoyed his version of a human workout. He climbed out of the water and shed his Selkie skin. He then hid his skin in one of the concealed crevices of the rock pillars. He dove back into the water in his human form and swam to shore to get the trunks he kept in the sea cave. Kendrick knew his Selkie pelt would be safe there as the waves crashed with such force that humans would not try to swim out to the rocks. Boats would never be able to come close to the pillars without colliding with the sharp, jagged quartzite.

The pillars had long been a safe place to stash the Selkie clan skins when his clan wanted to leave their seal form and walk as a human. Most of the Selkie males left a change of board shorts or trunks on the rock formation. The hidden trunks made walking out of the water easier to go to their cottages on the bluffs above. He chose to leave his swim trunks and a change of clothing in the small sea cave. The sea cave was accessible by land part of the time, hidden behind rocks which cloaked the entrance of the cave.

This area of the beach was the same place Kendrick had first run into Aileana. He still remembered their first meeting. He had been out in his Selkie form with a raft of seals and other male Selkies swimming and having a good time. He'd swum to shore to change and had just walked out of the sea cave when he saw a young human lass. The lush, long length of her hair was a dark, seductive auburn color, which brought to mind the fiery flow of molten lava. Her eyes were dark green that made him think of cool rich emeralds. Her peach-colored, pouty lips looked as sweet as the fruit that came to his mind. He remembered thinking she would be a heartbreaking beauty when she became an adult, woman.

She saw Kendrick first and waved her hand in greeting. The young lass had the most unusual accent and a way of speaking, which he'd never heard before. The lass told him she was from an area near Los Angeles. She was visiting her grandmother who lived on the cliffs in crofter cottage. They talked and swam each day for the rest of her visit and became friends. She had a feisty but sweet disposition with a fearless heart. The lass told him about the work her father did at the ocean research facility along the California coast. Also about her father's yearly trips to other parts of the world to study different oceans' marine organisms and their ecosystems.

She'd gone into detail regarding her surfing adventures with her friends in Malibu. Kendrick knew what surfing was. He just got little chance to see it on the Northern coasts of Scotland. There were a few hardy souls who braved the weather and waves up around Thurso. He'd heard that the power of the waves rolling in from the Pentland Firth compared with those of Hawaii—a place he hoped to visit someday. She was an interesting young lass; she possessed a mind which was inquisitive and astute.

He had nearly forgotten about the long-ago meeting until that evening he'd pulled her from the water. He still didn't put it together until he saw the necklace hanging between her full round breasts—it had the large pink, teardrop pearl. The young bonnie lass had vanished and in her place stood a breathtaking woman.

Now as he walked out the sea cave and into the light with his mind replaying his past encounter. He saw Aileana walking from the direction of the huge boulders on the beach. Kendrick could feel the tension and fear rolling off her body. He looked at the shoreline to see what danger could be near and saw nothing that should cause such fear. His protective instincts kicked into overdrive at the thought of Aileana in danger, possibly from one of the Finfolk.

"Bheag cailin, little girl, what has ye so fearful?"

Aileana replied, "I need you to tell me the truth about something important."

He worried about what she wanted to know. What could be so important and had made her so upset? Aileana trembled and tears streaked her cheeks. He couldn't understand what could be so terrible to upset her so. Kendrick wondered if it had to do with her story on the oil rigs. Did she need him to come clean about what he knew about the deals the oil men were making to bring more rigs into the area?

Aileana cried, "I have to know if I am on the verge of crazy town or not? I saw you leave the rock formation and swim to shore and go to the cave to get your trunks on."

"Seeing me naked, why would that upset ye so? I often swim naked when I think there is nay one on the beach. Surely ye have seen a nude man!"

"Of course I have seen men nude! I'm talking about before you dove back into the ocean. I saw a seal climb up upon the rocks and remove his skin to become a man! That man I saw dive into the water was you! Are you a Selkie, Kendrick? Are the folk tales my seanmhair told me as a child true?"

"Aye, lass, I am a Selkie, but it's crucial ye must nae speak of this to others. We Selkies are an ancient race that has lived among humans since the dawn of life on this planet. There are lots of myths aboot us. Some are true and some are nae."

"I think my seanmhair has known about your people."

"Yes, she kens aboot us."

"How and what does my *seanmhair* know about your people?"

"That is her story to tell, nae mine."

"Please explain to me about you and your people to help me to understand,"

"Have a seat on the sand this will take some time to tell ye. I will do my best to try to explain to ye aboot my Selkie clan. First, we live on the land as well as the sea. It is our choice. Most of the Selkies reside on the land and exist, most of the time in a humanoid form. There are those Selkies that have lost most of their humanity and are always in their Selkie form. Our clan is a branch of the Seelie court of ancient Selkies and enjoys contact with humans, unlike other Fin Folk who belong to the Unseelie court."

She stood up and started to pace along the shoreline. "What about the tales of stolen pelts? Is that true?"

He said, "Aye, and nay, tis true that the pelts can be stolen. But we are always able to locate them when we want them. They sing to our soul because they are alive and part of us. The only true way to be parted from our skins is if they're destroyed by the individual Selkie or by someone else."

"So the tales of Selkie wives that leave their human husbands when they find their skins is not correct?"

"The wives that leave are just like the land women. If yer human or Selkie male does nae treat ye weel, why would ye want to stay?"

"For their children!" she cried.

"Oh, aye the bairns, when we have bairns with humans, there is always a fifty-fifty chance they will be humans only."

"How do you know if they are Selkie or human?"

He walked over to a boulder on the sand, had a seat, and continued on with his explanation. He could tell she realized he wasn't pleased to have to explain to her about his Selkie clan, but he enlightened her just the same.

"The bairns born to be Selkies, most of the time, have slight webbing in their hands between their fingers. The webbing is tiny and delicate, but the only true test is when the wean is seven years old. The Selkie parent takes the child out in the ocean to swim. If the child is a Selkie, they will have a feeling of warmth come over them, and then the pelt will appear for the first time. Part of our Selkie magic," he replied.

"Is it always like that first change or shift of shape for you?"

"Nay, just the first, and then the rest of our lives we must have our pelt with us to transform back into our Selkie shape. To make the change to Selkie, the first transformation must be done in the seventh year of our life. There is no possibility of the Selkie change if not done in that year."

"I just have one more question for now. Do Selkies have the same life span as humans do? I ask because you do not appear to have aged since the first time we met twelve years ago."

"Nay, we live much longer. We can live over four hundred of yer human years. We only start to show age in the last thirty or so years of our life. I think that is because we are nae a prolific race of creatures, even taking into the account our children with humans. Less than fifty percent of all bairns born to the union of a Selkie and human are destined to be Selkie. With all the dangers of the sea, that may account why Selkies have a longer lifespan." he explained.

He then said to her, "Please don't let this change yer affections regarding us. What is happening between us is real, Aileana. I'm still the same being ye knew as a young lass and who you know now that you're grown. I have feelings for ye." He shared the details of his brother's death to help her understand their family's dynamics.

"I also should mention, now that we're being truthful with each other, that mah *athair* is the Lord of the Selkies from the Outer Hebrides to the North Sea. I will someday be Lord of the Selkies when mah *athair* steps down as I am next in line. I will be the Lord because of Callum death."

Aileana said, "I need to leave now. I need time to process this Selkie thing! I need time to myself and I also want to talk to my *seanmhair*. If I didn't see you change forms out on the rocks, I would say one of us is doing heavy duty drugs. You needn't worry about me talking to anyone other than my *seanmhair* since you said she knows about your people. I am categorically not ready for anyone to commit me to a mental hospital."

He watched her walk away. Part of him wished that he could walk away from her to make her life easier, but he knew, in his heart, that wasn't going to be possible. He felt the pull of his heart and their connection when he was near or far from Aileana, distance made no difference. The feeling was as though there was a tether from Aileana to himself. He wondered if she sensed their connection. He had not planned to have the complication of a life mate, but sometimes life makes the choice for us.

Chapter 14

Aileana

She needed to think and try to understand all Kendrick tried to explain to her. This unbelievable fact that she now knew existed, and not just in her *seanmhair's* tales of Selkie folklore. It would have been a fanciful fairy tale if she hadn't seen Kendrick climb up on the pillars out beyond the breakers. To witness his transformation from a seal to man; seeing him remove his Selkie skin and stand there upon the rocks a naked man was unsettling, to say the least. Aileana tried to wrap her brain around the facts he was a Selkie and his family's next ruler, which brought her to the shoreline on this moonlit night. The sound of the waves lapping against the shore seemed to soothe her frantic mind.

He'd told her he was born the second son to Murdock Morgan, the ruler of the Selkies off the northern coast of Scotland, she was aware of this part of his story. Because Murdock's firstborn son was killed back some five years ago, which was the reason Kendrick would be the next Selkie ruler. Before she had left the beach Kendrick told her about his brother's death. Callum, his older brother, had been shot by a roughneck out on an oil rig. The men were drunk and in their stupor thought shooting seals who were within range of the rig was a game. They shot his brother while he was in his Selkie form before their company man found out the idiots were out on the drilling platform drinking and shooting the wildlife.

The men were fired and taken off the rig the next day, but they had no idea of the horrendous act they had committed. Aileana couldn't begin to understand how difficult it must be to lose a loved one to a stupid cruel act. Even if the men didn't know they had killed someone's brother. It wasn't as if they had planned to eat their kill because their family needed food. It was just an act of malicious cruelty. She felt such overwhelming grief for Kendrick and his family.

She still didn't know which was harder to comprehend, that he was a Selkie or that he was a Selkie lord-to-be. This was a tremendous amount of information to process. Her world had now tilted on its axles and she needed to process and deal with it. *Yeah, right. Whatever.*

Her attraction to Kendrick was harder to fight each time she saw him. When she came here this year to Scotland she had only wanted to see her *seanmhair* and work through her pain from the breakup with her ex-boyfriend. Aileana sought out work in this corner of the globe. The trip here had been with the intention of making a break from the members of the male species. She hadn't had the best of luck with men lately. Aileana started to think all men were sketchy. She needed to bail out on the whole dating situation before she ended up swimming with *the men in the gray suits.*

She thought back to the time coming home to the house she shared in California. Aileana had arrived home early one day to see Paul-Mark, her live-in boyfriend at the time, with another woman, having wild sex in their living room. When she walked in the door, he'd been busy pounding into the other woman's body. He didn't realize Aileana stood in the living room with a stunned look on her face at the scene in front of her. He gave a loud groan as he had his orgasm and then realized Aileana stood in the same room. He jumped up and tried to tell Aileana, the woman meant nothing to him.

"From where I'm standing it sure looked like it meant something," she told him.

A Selkie's Magic

She tried to keep calm and let him know that it was over between them and she would be moving out the next day. She didn't want him to know how much he had destroyed her heart. Aileana drove to her parents' home and told them she would be staying with them for a while, and she then proceeded to cry buckets of tears.

For the next few days, she felt sorry for herself and wallowed in her grief. After the third day, she decided that she would put on her big girl panties and pull herself together. Aileana knew she just needed some time to get over the arrogant cheating jerk. She had always told herself everything happened for a reason, even if the reason made little sense at the time and hurt like hell. She knew it would hurt less in six months, and she now just had to get through those next six months. Her life would get better and no one would ever have the chance to hurt her in that way again, she would make sure of that.

So after licking her wounds for a few months at her parents' home, she decided to make her grandmother's home in Scotland her base of operation for the next year or so. She could live anywhere and still work as long as there is an internet connection to keep in touch with her editor at the magazine.

Aileana now knew part of the reason she'd been so drawn to Kendrick. He was the one male who had treated her as an adult. She was now sure he'd been aware of her schoolgirl crush twelve years ago. Even as a young girl she understood that he was a decent and kind human, or so she thought human. She thought to herself, *Let's just stick to the facts, a decent and kind male.* That wonderful summer she'd had the attention of someone older than herself. She had wondered if he was in his twenties. Little did she know that he was a hundred and thirty-five-year-old Selkie! As she had just now come to find out, a hundred-year-old Selkie was considered a young adult in the term of their life span. Kendrick explained that they were able to live up to four or five hundred years. No wonder he appeared the same as when she met him back twelve years ago. She just thought he'd been blessed with good genetics.

He told Aileana that many Selkies had human lovers but seldom took a human as their life mate. Humans were drawn to a Selkie's magic and beauty. Selkies were able to feel the emotions of the land dwellers. They wanted to comfort and heal wounded hearts and souls of the humans that were drawn to the ocean shores in a time of sorrow. The few Selkies who take human lovers and have children with them often, take the children and disappear back out to the sea, not to be seen again. Selkies only stayed with a human lover who was their life mate.

Aileana decided she needed a long walk by the moonlit seashore; walking tended to be extremely cathartic. She thought a walk would help her put the facts in some kind of perspective; any kind would help at this point in time. Didn't she want to run away? Just escape from such a tangled convoluted situation? She couldn't even imagine why she wasn't running as fast as she was able. What happened to the woman who'd sworn she wanted no involvement with men in the near foreseeable future? Little had Aileana ever imagined that when she came to Scotland she would run into her teenage crush.

In the twelve years since she'd met Kendrick, not once did she see him or hear of him when she came to Scotland each year. Aileana had all but forgotten him, except for the beautiful pearl he'd given her.

Her walk along the shore with the water lapping at her feet did make her feel calmer and seemed to bring some peace to her mind. The strong, steady pull of the moon on the water was just gravity at work, but seemed like magic with its hypnotic cadence. Just like the pull, she felt toward Kendrick.

A Selkie's Magic

Maybe Selkies and their magic were something which happened to be what it was and nothing more. The only questions were about what has not been explained, not what is already known. It would seem some things just defied rational thinking since Selkies appeared to be real—in fact. The Selkies prefer the world not to know of their existence. Didn't the world just newly discover an unknown tribe in the Amazon rainforest a few years back? The people of the world weren't aware of everything there was to understand about the planet.

Aileana realized Kendrick was still the same being that she knew twelve years ago, and the same being she had a chance to get reacquainted with now. She was not the type of person who would just put a label on a group of individuals and not try to understand them. She was proud to think she wasn't narrow-minded, but open-minded, a liberal, receptive to understanding all people. *We are all God's creatures in one way or another.*

She guessed her walk along the shore was a good idea as she now felt a calmness, which took over her mind and gave her a clearer understanding of the knowledge Kendrick shared with her. Aileana would now say she was one of the lucky few to have this knowledge. She still wanted to talk to her *seanmhair* and find out what she could tell her about the Selkies and how she knew about them. Her *seanmhair* was a lot like her, in that she was a "straight-shooter," very honest and direct with her answers.

Aileana decided then that she would go and try to find Kendrick first to let him know that after some time and a lot of reflecting on his information, she was sorry that she had reacted so awfully. She understood in her heart that Kendrick was a decent and kind being. Those were the most important qualities anyone could wish for in a lover.

So she walked farther down the beach, then up the walkway to his cottage that he had pointed out to her on one of their walks. She knew she could do this, but it still didn't make it easier.

Her heart was racing, but not because of knowing he was a Selkie. It raced at the thought of him as the male she was drawn to. She didn't know if this strong attraction she felt was because of him, or if it was some sensual Selkie magic. Just thinking of Kendrick made her stomach and insides clench with want and need.

She needed to let Kendrick know that she wanted to see where their path would take them. She wanted him to understand that she would try to wrap her mind around the whole Selkie thing. She didn't comprehend all the ins and outs of the Selkie race, but she wanted to learn and understand. This information was a life changer if she continued her relationship with Kendrick. How would this affect her life and her family? Perhaps her *seanmhair* would be able to shed more light on her questions.

Chapter 15

Kendrick

Aileana stood gazing at the moon over the dark water looking so bonnie in the moonlight. She made his heart pound as no other woman or Selkie female ever had. Kendrick was drawn to her now, just as he was when she was a young teenage lass. Only now the years had passed and he could act upon those emotions. His thoughts brought him to the conclusion he would make her his in body and soul. Her willful nature was a challenge that called to him. She would be strong and stand at his side to rule his clan with him.

He watched her turn away from the sea and walk toward his cottage up on the hill. He took a different path to meet her at his cottage so she wouldn't realize he'd been watching her as she walked along the shore. She knocked tentatively on the front door.

Kendrick approached her. "What brings ye here this time of night?"

"I came to apologize about how badly I reacted to the news that you're a mythological creature." There was a smile on her lips. "You just never know how you're going to take astonishing news until you're the one receiving it. I did some thinking about what you said, and I realized you're the same man or male, I know, or whatever! I'm aware something is happening between us, and I feel we need to see where it leads us. I don't know about you, but I feel this kind of tugging on my feelings toward you. It is hard for me to explain it as I have never felt it before. It is as if this is where I need to be—with you." She said it in a rush, trying to say everything all once. Perhaps before she could change her mind.

That was all he needed to hear from her as he took her hips and pulled her close to his body, she felt so small tucked up against him. He felt the swell of her breasts against his chest. Her nipples pebbled against him. His hard length pressed into her stomach; he knew she could feel his need and desire for her. He bent down to taste her luscious mouth. He explored her lips, which were so soft and plump, waiting for him to make her his. Their lips fit together like pieces of a puzzle. Kendrick moved his tongue to the seam of her mouth to savor her nectar. His tongue lightly probed until she opened for him. Then he slid in her lush mouth to taste her sweetness within. He could sense her tongue was as curious as his to touch and take as they collided and tangled with each other.

His hands skimmed up her hips to the small waist he could span easily. She moved closer to him so his rigid length pressed against her flat belly. Kendrick's hands moved up around her full breasts and palmed them to explore their weight. Her nipples tightened further as he pinched the rosy peaks.

With his other hand, he pushed the door to the cottage open and guided her into his cozy, warm home. His home was lit only by the glow of the peat burning in the fireplace. He gathered her in his arms and carried her small form inside. He placed her on her feet in front of the fire on the sheepskin rug. They stood looking into one another's eyes, and he saw the passion which lay just beneath the surface of her beautiful face.

As their eyes were locked together, he took a few moments so they could catch their breath. "Aileana, ye know I want ye. I need to know if this is something that ye want, too. I want to make love with ye. I need to be inside of ye. If you're not ready, I need to stop now before I can't. Yer all I've been thinking of since ye came back to the village."

"Kendrick, I did a lot of thinking, and not just about you being a Selkie. I also thought about the feelings I have when I am with you. I have had you on my mind more than I will admit since you spilled my drink on me in the pub. I want to see if this is more than a leftover schoolgirl crush." She smiled. "I want you, Kendrick."

He reached for her again and she came to him willingly and melted into his body. As he sampled her mouth once again, she ignited such a fire within him, it was difficult to not to rush. He wanted her to experience the need just as much as he was consumed with his, the need to be with her.

They made love with their tongues, and he slid her sweater up her body and over her head. He pulled it off in one quick move so he could feel her skin next to his. He slowly moved his hand to the front of her black lace bra to unclasp it so her full young breasts would spill into his waiting hands. Kendrick heard her sigh as his mouth traveled down her neck. He licked and bit his way to her beautiful full globes.

He suckled at each breast in turn so they would know the feel the brand of his mouth and tongue. He lapped at each nipple; they got much harder and fuller, wanting and waiting his attention. As he laved each breast he could feel the beat of her racing heart, keeping time with his own. There was no doubt whether they would make love, they were each driven by their inner animal to do what nature demanded.

Chapter 16

Aileana

She was so overwhelmed with the emotions that Kendrick brought out in her, she wondered if it was the feelings she had for him since she was a young girl or if it was part of his Selkie enchantment. At the moment, there was no more time to try to figure out everything he had told her in regards to the Selkies and their very existence.

His kisses made her feel vibrantly alive, more so than she ever thought possible. He carried her inside his warm cottage, kissing and touching her the whole way to the fireplace with its low burning fire. He tasted fresh and clean against her tongue; she couldn't get enough of him. He had a spicy intoxicating scent that she couldn't place, but it drew her to him as if she'd been drugged.

He placed her on something warm and fuzzy under her feet. He stopped and held her close as he asked if she was sure this was what she wanted, if she was ready to take this step. She looked up at him and nodded as she said the words.

She glanced down to see a white fur rug, which he beckoned her to lie on. Before she could act on that suggestion, she gazed into his eyes and became lost in those enchanting dark pools. His eyes were saying so much to her without words, she felt as if she would drown in desire. Their mouths collided once again and she felt his hands move slowly down her body to the front of her jeans. He undid the button and slid the zipper down. That would have been the time to put the brakes on their passion if she was going to try and do the logical thing, but it seemed as though her judgment had taken a backseat to her need. She would just have to worry about all those troublesome questions later.

Kendrick turned her toward the fire, backed her up against the massive expanse of his hard naked chest, and pulled her tight against his body. She could feel his desire, rigid and full against her lower spine as he started kissing and nibbling his way down her neck while reaching around and unsnapping her bra.

She heard him groan softly as her breasts fell into his palms. He gently squeezed her nipples and tugged on them, making her wet with her need for him. His hands slipped lower into her jeans. He went straight to her core and slid his thick finger into her wet sex.

Her legs felt weak and wobbly, and if it weren't for him holding her against his body, she would have slid to the floor. As he moved his finger deep inside her, his thumb strummed a different melody on her clit. His mouth once again ravished her mouth; his hard driving tongue was giving her a preview of what was to come. All it took was a few more moments of his exquisite torture to take her to the edge and over the cliff to one of the best orgasms of her life.

He slid her pants down her hips, and she pushed her feet out of her boots and the denim pants dropped to the floor. Aileana turned to face him and reached to undo the buttons on the fly of his Levi's. The evidence of his arousal was right under her fingers as she unbuttoned his pants.

He wore the perfect underwear—none. She loved how he'd gone commando. Nothing was hotter than seeing his cock leap up out of his pants' fly. She slid them off and got her first full close-up view of his muscular body. Her mouth was the perfect level to reach out and run her tongue over his flat, hard nipples. They pebbled and his passion was stoked by her tongue as she tasted him. Aileana was aware that he enjoyed her attention to his sculpted chest as much as she loved the feel of him. She licked him from his navel down his solid taut stomach with ridges of hard muscles, down to his breathtaking, thick cock. His thick length was hard with his arousal and its large flared head glistened with pre-cum at his slit. She took the tip of his shaft and licked and tasted his salty sweetness. She couldn't seem to get enough of him in her mouth, but she sure gave it a good try.

She felt him reach down and caress her hair; then reached lower to pull her up all the way to his hot mouth. She held him and sensed Kendrick holding himself in check as his body raged to possess her. She could feel his muscles as they bunched beneath her fingertips, hear his moans as they grazed over his tight ass. He gently took her to the floor and started his exploration of her body with his large gentle hands and warm wet mouth.

Once again his fingers found her drenched sex and slid inside to her slick inner folds. His wet fingers moved to caress her swollen bud, which throbbed with her desire and her need for release, he kept her on the threshold of ecstasy. He was building her release to a crescendo and then backing off, prolonging the exquisite torment between pain and pleasure. She started to beg him to give her the release she craved; she needed that release as she needed her next breath. He moved his body to cover hers and took his thick cock in hand.

He asked, "Is this what ye want"?

"Please, give me every inch of your cock. I need you now. Wait! Do you have a condom?"

"I cannae give ye any diseases. Selkies don't have any, and we cannae transfer any human diseases. I cannae get ye with child unless I want to, and I won't do that to ye without yer permission. I need to stroke and be inside ye without a condom so that I may experience all of ye. Is that okay with ye?"

She could only nod yes. Kendrick moved slowly to let her adjust to his thickness and length. His shaft slid inside her tightness, he was so huge that it was on the painful side of pleasure for her. Her body clenched as her insides heated; she craved what he so generously gave her. He was now buried all the way to her core; he stopped to let her get used to his size before starting to rock back and forth building up a faster rhythm that matched the tattoo of their heartbeat. She was close to the brink of her personal pinnacle; she begged him to make her release happen.

He reached between their bodies and brushed her clit. She exploded as he took a few more, hard, deep strokes before filling her body with his warm life essence. As he reached his own release she could see his black obsidian eyes reflecting the fire in the burning hearth, along with his blazing passion. Aileana was so sated and overcome with an extremely euphoric sensation. This aura must be part of the Selkie's magic she was bespelled with, and it was too strong to just to be his astonishing lovemaking.

Chapter 17

Kendrick

As Kendrick experienced the afterglow of their incredible sex he understood he had to let Aileana know she was now "his." Whether she knew it or not they were now bonded life mates. He knew from the time he saved her from drowning during the storm that there was a good chance she was going to be his mate, but he'd been unsure until he felt the fusion of their essences in shared sex. He could only hope she would be agreeable to sharing her life with him. He wondered how she would feel having a Selkie as a life mate. Without Aileana, his life would not be complete; there would never be true happiness with anyone else but his life mate. That was how it was with Selkies.

Selkies without a life mate could and did have sex with others—humans and other Selkies alike. Selkies were known for their prowess and sexual talents. But the Selkies that had life mates did not wander from their mates. They remained faithful until death. When a Selkie's life essence fused with one that was their life mate, it created an unbreakable bond. Many human women had found comfort from Selkies that found them crying by the seashore. It was untrue about the seven years and only seeing their Selkie lover once every seven years. That tale was started by the humans because the Seelie Court of Selkies wished to be kind and seek those who were dissatisfied with their love life. They knew that their passions and seductive ways always made the women or men forget their woes. But unless there was a bond in a life mate, a Selkie lover would not stay.

A Selkie's Magic

Selkies of the Unseelie Court were made up of darkly-inclined Selkies responsible for creating storms and sinking ships. The Unseelie Selkies did this to punish humans that had hunted or harmed other Selkies while in their seal form, or the indiscriminate slaughter of seals.

"*Céadsearc*, I need ye to wake so that we may speak of what is between us."

"What did you just call me, Kendrick?"

"I called ye 'first love'."

"First love, is that true or are you just telling me that?"

"Nay, it is true. I, in mah one hundred and thirty-five years of being alive, have never been in love before ye. I have cared but never felt this love I have for ye. To a Selkie, true love is a rare emotion. We are a race meant to always feel the passion and enjoy a joining, but real love is saved for a special few."

"I have a special affection for you also, but I am unsure if it is love. I gave my heart to someone before, and he betrayed me and hurt me badly. I just prayed that the time would pass quickly and lessen the pain he caused me. It appears I am still not over the awful memory, but I'm working on that situation."

"Mah beloved *céadsearc*, I will never hurt ye or cause ye any pain, I would die for ye, but now that we're bonded, we will have bairns."

"Someday I think I will want children, but that is for the future."

"Yer someday will be the next time we make love now that our essences have bonded. Unless I ken to not use or choose not to use mah Selkie magic you will get pregnant."

"What do you mean? What are you talking about, Kendrick? I am covered by my birth control shot."

"That is fine if ye were having sex with a human. With Selkie sex—once we find our life mate—the only way to prevent a pregnancy is if I control mah life force. All Selkie males are in charge of their life force. We can control it with our minds to mix it with our sperm when we want to impregnate a female. It is in our DNA, the need to procreate. It is nature's way of trying to increase our Selkie numbers. When we have sex with a woman who is our life mate those women have a much greater chance of having a bairn with us. We use our Selkie magic to make sure there is nay protection against a pregnancy. That is our way."

She asked in a small voice. "How many children do you have? Do I even want to know?"

"I dinnae have any human offspring that are still alive," he replied. "But I do have two children that are Selkies."

"Please explain what you mean by 'you don't have human offspring still alive'?"

"Well, the human offspring I have had are long since dead from old age. Our human offspring age as any human would, nay Selkie magic," he replied.

"What of the two Selkie children?"

"They're nae children any longer. Mah son Laird will be seventy-eight soon, mah daughter Kenzie is forty-nine years old now."

Chapter 18

Aileana

She walked back to the cottage after she spent the night in Kendrick's arms. His home was about a mile up the coast from her grandmother's. As she entered the cozy home, she was met with the smells of Scottish brown bread baking in her *seanmhair's* oven.

The fragrant aroma of the fresh bread took her back to her childhood summers in Scotland with her grandmother. She loved her *seanmhair's* wonderful Scot's country cooking and her folk tales, she just hadn't realized that some of the tales weren't fiction.

As Aileana moved to give her *seanmhair* good morning hug and kiss, Skye eyed her and said, "What has placed that smile upon yer face? Are ye just getting in, or were ye up early and just returned from a walk? This old lady is curious and wants to ken what mah *ban-ogha* is doing this bonnie morning."

Aileana sat at the small square table near the fireplace with her grandmother to enjoy their breakfast of warm brown bread with fresh sweet butter, Lorne sausage, and eggs. She chuckled to herself, thinking the Scots sure knew how to eat, and they ate big at breakfast time. She would have to make sure she got a daily jog in to keep from getting big as a walrus. It wasn't too hard to enjoy her runs on the beach next to the cliffs, and it was a fantastic way to keep the weight in check and the heart healthy after the substantial Scottish meals.

But now was the time to talk to her *seanmhair* about her stories of the Selkies. Aileana needed to find out what her *seanmhair* knew of the Selkies. She had thought the stories of Selkies were only fairy tales told to children; it turned out they weren't just folk tales.

"Tell me about the Selkies. I want to know what you know of them, *Seanmhair*."

She replied, "Have ye found yersel' a Selkie, *ban-ogha*? I once had an extraordinarily handsome Selkie choose me to be his life mate. We were happy for many years."

"*Seanmhair*, what do you mean you were his life mate? Does that make Daddy a Selkie if you had a life mate"?

"So ye do have a Selkie. Ye would have to have a Selkie to have knowledge about a life mate. Yes, yer father was a Selkie, but nay longer. He gave up his skin and his memories of his Selkie life when he decided to marry yer mother."

"Does Mom know that Daddy was a Selkie? Why would he give up his skin and not be a Selkie any longer?"

"Yer mother has no idea yer father was once a Selkie, and he has no memory of being a Selkie either. The reason was love, not just the love for yer mother, but also for the work he was doing with the Ocean Research Center in Malibu. He felt he could make more of a contribution to the Selkies by living on the land. He wanted to make a difference with the knowledge he had gained as a Selkie."

Her *seanmhair* went on to tell Aileana that by destroying his skin he would not be able to return to the sea as a Selkie. Also by destroying his pelt, he would not have any memories of ever being a Selkie. He still kept his knowledge of the sea, but not the understanding of how he knew it. It made it much easier to live as a human if you had no memory of your prior life. What her father had done was a big sacrifice, which few Selkies would ever do.

She asked her *seanmhair* to tell her about her Selkie grandfather and what had actually happened to him? Did he leave her and go back to the sea, even though she was his life mate? This new knowledge of her family's roots was astonishing, to say the least.

"Weel, mah story began when I was dancing at our local highland games. It was the year I turned sixteen. While I was on stage, I noticed a huge young man striding toward the edge of the stage. This stranger was so handsome with his long black hair, and there was something about him that drew my eyes to him."

"So, *Seanmhair*, was he was a guy from the village?"

"Nay, I had never seen him before, I would have remembered such a tall handsome man. He watched me as if he knew who I was. At first, I was somewhat nervous because his eyes never wavered while he watched me as I continued my dance."

"So what happened, what did he say to you, *Seanmhair*?"

Her grandmother started to laugh as she continued her story. "After I finished my dance and walked off the stage, he strode over to me big as ye, please. He then looked me in the eyes with those dark brown eyes of his, and he said the most outrageous statement to me. He told me he'd had a vision of meeting a bonnie, green-eyed lass, with long auburn curls that would become his mate."

"Oh, that sounds like something I would hear coming out of Kendrick's mouth. It must be a Selkie thing." She laughed at the thought of her grandfather making such a bold declaration.

"Yer grandfather courted and wooed me, then he won mah parents' approval. Mah parents understood mah Mackenzie Sutherland wasn't going to take no, fur an answer. Mah parents said yes because they could see how much he loved me. He also promised to buy a cottage near the village, so I would never be far from mah parents. Even then this was a big step for a sixteen-year-old lass."

"Did you know he was a Selkie then?"

"Nay, I didn't find out till mah wedding night. He explained what being a Selkie meant, he also told me that because I was his life mate he would never leave me to return to the sea. He bought this cottage I live in now because it is so close to the ocean. That by living here he would be able to take short Selkie swims. And that would be enough for him as long as he had me," she said with a wistful smile.

"*Seanmhair*, I hope I haven't upset you with all my questions?"

"Aileana, that was the most incredible and blissful part of mah life. I was then blessed again when our son, yer father Iain was born. After yer father's seventh birthday it became clear Iain was also a Selkie. Yer father loved going out with Mackenzie in his boat, yer grandfather fished to make a living for us. Plus every once in a while he'd find gold coins off the shore, in ancient ships that had gone down in storms long ago."

"That explains a lot why Dad loves the sea so much."

"Yer father, even as a young *balach*, he dreamed of becoming an oceanographer to study plants and animals in the sea. He wanted to make a difference to humans and to his father's Selkie Clan."

"What happened to my grandfather?"

"Mackenzie had made a trip inland to deliver his fresh-caught fish to the Hotel Lairg's restaurant. On the ninety-minute trip back home, some young people took a bend in the road and swung wide hitting Mackenzie's vehicle head-on. No one survived the crash." As Skye told her story her arms wrapped around herself as if to give her comfort at losing her Selkie husband.

"*Seanmhair*, you must have been rather young when all this happened? Did you ever think about remarrying?" Aileana asked.

"I was only thirty-three years old back when it happened, and yer father a young *balach* of twelve. Iain lost his father, but I lost mah best friend, mah lover and mah life mate. After Mackenzie's death, I worked in one of the restaurants in town making baked goods. I did try dating later on, but no one could take his place in mah heart."

Chapter 19

Kendrick

The evening before, Kendrick asked Aileana to spend the day with him. He told her he wanted to show her Scotland's bonnie highland countryside. He wanted to spend the time to get to know her better. She thought that would be a wonderful idea and she would be ready the next morning for their little adventure.

The next morning he grabbed the extra black helmet he stashed in the cabinet by his front door. He locked his front door and walked over to his newest baby—his Harley-Davidson Street Glide Special. She was a fiery red color he called "Dorothy's Ruby Red Slippers." The Harley Davidson people called the color Mysterious Red Sunglo; he liked his color name better. She was a smooth bagger-style bike that was as cool as a tall glass of ice water on a scorching hot day.

He had one stop to make before he headed over to pick up Aileana. He went into a small restaurant bar in town. He placed an order for a couple of sandwiches and fruit to go along with a couple bottles of water. This was where having a bagger-style bike came in handy.

Kendrick needed to feed Aileana to keep up her strength for what he planned for the day, and he thought, *What woman doesn't like a picnic*? He pulled up in front of her grandmother's cottage and turned off his sweet ride. As he removed his helmet and placed it on the handlebars of the bike, he turned to see her grandmother approach.

Skye walked toward him from around the side yard where she'd been working in her vegetable garden. She removed her muddy garden gloves and stuck out her hand. She said, "Hello, ye must be Kendrick. Aileana has been talking to me about ye. I knew yer parents a long time ago. Murdock and Fiona, right?" "Aye, that's right," he said.

"How are they getting on? It seems like a lifetime ago we were friends." She sighed.

"They are doing great; my màthair has grandchildren now that my sister has taken a life mate. And my *athair* is always busy with the care of our clan business and driving me and mah brother crazy over one thing or another." He laughed.

"Well, it looks like there's going to be some changes around here, now that mah *banogha* is aware of yer people."

"Dinna fash, I will make sure she is taken care of and happy. Do you have any regrets when it came to being yer Mackenzie's life mate?"

"Och! Heavens no! No regrets about having the most wonderful, handsome man in my life. And I was given a perfect gift of having Iain as my son, and now mah *banogha's*, Aileana and Adaira. I have had a rich life. Mah only wish was I still had mah, Mackenzie, to share it with. As it is with being married to a human or a Selkie, there are no guarantees how long we are on this earth. We all need to just grab onto our happiness and enjoy every moment we have it. Now, let this old woman get back to her garden, and I will go get Aileana for you. Ye take care of mah *banogha* on yer wicked-looking motorcycle, ye hear me?"

"As they say in the States, 'No problem'." He winked at her and laughed.

He leaned up against the bike and crossed his boot-clad feet, thinking he may be in for a wait, but to his surprise, as her grandmother went in the door, Aileana came out. She was a bonnie vision. Her auburn curls were long and loose as they gleamed in the morning sunlight. She wore next to no makeup except some peach-colored lip gloss; it made him want to taste her lush full lips. She was dressed in well-worn 501 jeans and a black knit Henley shirt with the sleeves pushed up to the elbow. She also had on a dark brown Sorel's and carried in her hand a black L.A. Kings baseball cap.

She was a collection of contradictions, dressed in jeans and hiking boots with all her lush feminine curves. Aileana wasn't aware of the strong reaction Kendrick's body had when he was with her, even when she was dressed casual and natural. She was so beautiful without even trying, unlike all the previous women he had been with in his long life. Her natural look was her beauty. It took all his control not to grab her and throw her down on the ground and pleasure her. His animal wanted loose.

She glanced over to where he rested against the bike seat and let out a *whoop*. She then bounded down the steps. She seemed more excited by the Harley than touring the highlands. Now he loved that bike, but like most males he wanted to be the focus of her attention, not the damn bike. She must have seen the look on his face as it gave away his thoughts.

She said, "Get over yourself, dude. I have always loved bikes. As a kid, my dad bought my sister and me trail bikes to ride with him when he wasn't working on some ocean research project or another. Every couple of years Dad would buy us a bigger bike until we finally could keep up with him. We wanted to do the whole motocross racing thing when we were in our teens, but Mom put the kibosh on that."

"Okay, good to ken! Ye're just full of surprises, aren't ye?"

She laughed as she replied, "You betcha, red rider."

"All right, let's get this show on the road as ye yanks say." Kendrick pulled her to his body and handed her a helmet, then kissed her lips soundly, which promised much more.

A Selkie's Magic

They climbed on his bike and started up the lane toward the A838 road. Their first stop was the small village of Scourie on the North West coast, about twenty-five miles down the road. He enjoyed the Scottish countryside with her holding on tight to him, her head sometimes lying against his back. They continued on down to Loch Shin, where he thought they could get off, in more ways than one, and work out some of their kinks.

He pulled off the road in a shady wooded area by the loch, out of the sightline from the road. Kendrick found a sheltered spot under some trees at the edge of the loch. He grabbed a blanket from the saddlebag on the bike; he anticipated putting the blanket to good use. She looked at him with a sly smile when she saw he had prepared ahead of the ride.

"What do you have planned for that blanket? I don't think I need a nap."

"I have all kinds of *mean, evil, wicked, bad, nasty* things planned. Now, come here.

Yer Selkie lover needs ye and that sweet body of yers."

"Only if you can catch me, Mr. Selkie!" She dodged between the trees, laughing the whole time.

Now this was a game he excelled in. The predator in him loved a good chase. He was fast in and out of the water. He thought he took her by surprise as he easily chased her down and effortlessly scooped up his laughing auburn-haired beauty. Her laugh was infectious and he couldn't help laughing along with her. Now that he had acquired his prize, he wanted his reward. He carried her over to the blanket and gently placed her there.

His mouth nibbled at her ear, and he started to slide his lips down the side of her neck. He gently nipped all the way down the slender column. As her moans of pleasure started to rise in volume they drove him insane with his desire. He needed to ravish her body and soul just to hear her scream his name in the heat of passion. Kendrick reached out to palm her full breasts, felt her nipples tighten into hard peaks beneath his hands. He grasped the bottom of her knit top and raised it slowly, taking in the beauty of her silky, smooth skin, taking his time to savor every sensuous curve. Kendrick pulled her shirt up and over her head and drank in the sight of her plump, firm breasts confined in a red lace bra. He could see her large pale pink areolae through the red lace. He started licking her nipples within the lace of her bra.

She held his head and gripped his hair for all she was worth. He needed more. He released her mounds of lushness from her bra so his mouth could suck her hard peaks. Kendrick pulled each stiff peak in turn, into his mouth and suckled as if he was ravenous. He unbuttoned her 501s and slid them down her lush hips. He removed her boots and socks from her small soft feet with bright red toe polish and massaged her high arches. His hands started up her lightly tanned legs, caressing and stroking as he went higher. His mouth followed his hands, licking and tasting her. Her skin tasted sweet on his tongue and her natural fragrance of honeyed spice filled his senses. Her sweet sighs filled his ears and made his cock so hard he felt as though it would burst through his pants. His rigid shaft needed to be out of his pants, and he wanted to be inside of her snug wet pussy.

Today was going to be all about Aileana. He wanted her as he had never wanted another female, ever. He wanted to brand her body with his sex and make her crave him as he craved her.

"*Mo nighean*, my lass, let me love ye."

"Please, Kendrick, I want you now. I can't wait to feel you inside me, filling me, stretching me," she whispered.

"*Mo nighean ruadh*, let me show ye how wondrous, it's possible to feel with yer Selkie lover," he replied.

He stood and removed his shirt. Toed off his boots and removed his pants and socks. Kendrick's erection bounced against his belly as the blue jeans dropped to the ground. His shaft was as hard as the drilling pipes on the oil rigs. The head of his cock pulsated and was deep purple-red with his arousal, the slit glistened with his pre-cum.

Kendrick dropped to his knees and lowered himself to the ground. He parted her thighs and lowered his mouth between her silky-smooth legs. He breathed in her honeyed scent.

"Yer scent is what I'm sure must be the fragrance of heaven," he told her.

Her arousal glistened in evidence on her swollen pink nether lips. He pulled her lower lips apart, and he lowered his mouth to taste her sweet cream, savoring her as his tongue lapped at her wet folds, capturing her moisture. His tongue wanted to reach deep into her tight wet opening to give her a preview of what his cock would be doing soon.

She gripped his hair and pulled him tighter into her sweet sex. His tongue zeroed in on her swollen clit and lapped at her hypersensitive bud with steady unrelenting strokes. He moved his finger inside her drenched core and felt her tension build as he used his tongue to flick her clit to an explosive climax.

He felt her orgasm, the strong contractions convulsing in her tight body. He moved up her body and placed his cock at her entrance and rubbed her abundant cream on the head of his shaft. Her wetness eased the way for him to gradually slide his thick cock in. Kendrick's mouth took possession of her lips and he slipped his tongue into her mouth so she would taste her nectar on his tongue.

He started the timeless movement of his hips. Slowly withdrawing from her body and then surging forward again over and over until he felt her start to writhe beneath him. Each time she got close to her peak, Kendrick slowed the surge of his hips to prolong her ecstasy. He used a small amount of his Selkie magic to make sure he didn't blow his load until he brought her to her peak. Aileana began to plead that she wanted him to pound her harder and faster. Kendrick needed this lovemaking to be the most intense she'd ever experienced.

Their sensuality was so extreme it bordered between pleasure and pain. She pleaded with him to give her the release she was so close to attaining. He reached between their bodies and pressed his finger against her clit in small, quick circles as he started to thrust deeper and harder. He felt her shudder as she reached another orgasm and let loose with a scream of satisfaction. He felt her inner muscles clamp down tight around his shaft as he rode out the waves of her climax. Then, he knew he could let himself go and join her in his own release. He felt his cock length and thicken; it started to jerk deep in her body. His release ripped through him and flooded her spasming channel.

A few moments later he held her tight and rolled over on his back taking her with him. Kendrick settled her against his chest, and they both drifted off to sleep with his cock still deep inside her.

After their brief nap, he woke her up and asked, "Are ye hungry, *mo maise*, my beauty?"

She squinted at Kendrick and she replied, "I think I will always be hungry for you, but as of now I am famished for some food." She smiled.

He raised his mouth to her and kissed her swollen lips. "I have a cure for that in mah saddlebags."

He grabbed his Levi's and slipped them on as he went to grab their lunch of sandwiches, fruit, and water.

"You certainly planned out our day, thinking of everything we might need. I am so glad we went on this excursion, Kendrick," she said as she pulled on her clothes.

A Selkie's Magic

After they finished their picnic lunch by Loch Shin, they climbed back on the bike for the two-hour trip back to Durness. They made a few stops to check out the views of the countryside on their return trip.

Chapter 20

Finman

He had kept the cottage on the hill in sight all night and knew that there were two humans in the dwelling. As the sun started to rise and the darkness faded, an older human female left the dwelling. She got into a small car and drove down the road toward town.

This was the time for him to abduct the young redheaded female. He didn't sense any other humans in the area, nor did he detect the presence of the large protective male Selkie either. The Finman walked up the steps from the beach, without making a sound, and he used his sorcery abilities to enter the cottage. Locked doors were no deterrent for Finfolk. He sensed where the human female was located in the dwelling and made his way to the room she occupied. The Finman smelled the Selkie, but only his scent—it was too faint to actually be him in the dwelling. The female smelled of the Selkie, and he could tell the Selkie had marked her. That knowledge changed his already ominous mood and made him want to inflict pain and destroy whatever got in his way.

The Finman could feel her presence beyond the door he stood in front of. He opened the door and spotted her small form under the quilts on the bed. He slunk to the bed to inspect her while she still slept. He reached and removed the covers off her body when her eyes started to open slowly. She screamed, but the Finman covered her mouth with one hand. With his other, he used his fist and connected with her jaw to knock her unconscious.

He hoisted her over his shoulder and moved out the door of the cottage. The Finman was down the stairway to the beach and out in the ocean before anyone was aware she had been taken. He swam with her some distance to where he had his small skiff anchored and threw her inert body to the bottom of the boat. The Finman pulled himself aboard and quickly tied her up before she came to. He ripped her clothes off and threw them overboard; he wanted to feast his eyes upon her naked body. The shape-shifter's mood changed considerably. Arousal stiffened his cock, which jerked and extended at the sight of her rounded curves, the plump, ripe tits with her pale nipples that had pebbled from being naked and wet. His gaze traveled to her small trimmed patch of dark red curls at her nether lips. He wanted to ravish her in every way known to his depraved species. He decided to wait till they were back on the Finfolk island of Hildaland, where he would use his magic to convince her to be his. He smiled to himself thinking of how he would use her and show her his world of pain. Thinking thoughts of her pain made his cock throb with need as he stroked himself.

On his island, he took her to his bedchamber and threw her across the bed. The Finman took his time binding her hands to the stone wall at the back of the bed and securing her spread legs to the end of the bed. He wanted to make her plead for her life, for her to realize he was in control and she would be his to do with as he pleased. He would use mind control to convince her to become his wife. She would bear his future heirs.

He watched her eyes sluggishly start to open.

As she came to, he said to her, "If you struggle those knots will only tighten."

Her eyes darted to the doorway where he stood. She gasped as she saw him. She became aware of her naked state, spread out like a smorgasbord, and his eyes were already feasting greedily on her. She fought the gag he'd placed in her mouth.

"I want you to understand there is no help for you now. I will leave you to your thoughts, so you may prepare yourself to accept me and what we will be doing together."

He lifted his hard massive cock for her frightened eyes to view and roughly stroked himself. He could see the tears stream from her eyes, which just made him harder as he fisted his phallus and continued to jack off. He shot his white-hot load over her struggling body and leered at her naked body with uncontrolled lust.

He contemplated how he would get the most pleasure with his newest prey. The longer he toyed with his prey the harder his enormous cock became. He wanted to see her terror in her eyes and smell the scent of her fear pour from her body. Fear was part of the thrill which made the rush much more visceral—it was part of the hunt, the games he would devise to play with his captive.

He sent the last slave, he had kidnapped to bring the new female some food and water. He told the slave to just feed her and give her water. She knew better than to untie redheaded woman. She realized he would kill her for the transgression if she loosened the captive's bonds. The beatings the Finman generously gave the young servant made her a docile slave. He was aware the pain kept her a more malleable wench.

The Finman left it to the slave to see to the redhead. He needed to take care of more pressing matters dealing with his Finfolk clan. There was no escape from the Finfolk shifting island; they would never find their way out of surrounding magical fog. They would die if they tried to escape.

Chapter 21

Aileana

Oh my God! I'm in a world of shit! That was an understatement of the facts, she thought. She was conscious enough to glance around. The walls of the room were a grimy gray and she didn't think the color came from a can of paint. The windows were without glass, mere slits in the walls. The filthy bed reeked of something she would rather not think about. There was one table with a chipped pitcher and what appeared to be some sort of a chamber pot in the corner.

Aileana heard a deep voice telling her not to fight the restraints which bound her to the walls above the bed she was lying on. Her ankles were also secured in a way which had her spread wide open in all respects. She also realized she was naked as the day she was born. Aileana wanted to give that piece of shit a few choice words from her not-so-ladylike mouth. If only she wasn't gagged with some sort of foul tasting rag, which made her want to puke.

Her eyes moved to follow his raspy voice. She gasped! There a ginormous specter came into her view. He was the same person who had snatched the young blonde woman from the beach. She knew it had been no lovers' quarrel—and just her damn luck—she was correct, for once she wished she'd been wrong. *Shit, shit! How did this happen?*

His soulless dark eyes were eating her alive; he devoured her body with those black unholy pits from hell. She couldn't even try to cover herself. He spoke again, but her brain didn't function as she saw him obscenely stroking and jerking his massive, erect cock.

God in heaven, please don't let him come any closer to me, she prayed. She couldn't stop the tears from running down her face as she came to terms with what the creature might have planned for her. Aileana was aware of how engorged his cock was getting and that he relished her tears even more. He was a sadistic beast. She did notice through her tears he wasn't human, but, in fact, was some sort of creature. What was he? Certainly not a Selkie! She examined his face instead of watching him beat his cock.

His face had a gaunt, skeletal shape. Even in the dim light, she was able to see his skin was pale. The lank brown hair that fell to his shoulders was matted in spots to his scalp. The hand not wrapped around his dick had pronounced webbing between the fingers.

The way he leered at her made her feel as though she was a mouse that some tomcat was toying with before he devoured his meal.

Aileana noticed his eyes start to close and his head lean back against the door frame. He started making grunting sounds as his hand, picked up speed and he shot his wad on the stone floor. He glared into her eyes and laughed as he recognized her terror.

He rubbed his junk a few more times and told her to think about what he would be doing with her when she decided to be his. *Did he just say when I decide to be his? That would happen when hell froze over,* she thought. As he turned away and walked out the doorway, Aileana heard him speak to someone in the next room, but she couldn't understand what he said.

Her mind raced trying to figure a way to escape this creature and place of horror. Her *seanmhair* wouldn't even know she was gone until late this evening or possibly not until the next day. She and a few of her friends were going to be busy planning the yearly Samhainn festival.

She wondered when Kendrick would even realize she was missing. They hadn't made any definite plans to meet. Even if he was aware she was gone, would he be able to find her? As her mind raced to try to find various answers to her dilemma, a dirty, bedraggled woman walked into the room carrying a tray with a chipped bowl. The woman came closer and started to take the gag from Aileana's mouth. The woman's frightened eyes darted around the room. Her lips were split in several places. Her left eye was partially swollen shut and bruises covered most of her body. The woman's nude body was only somewhat draped with a disgusting old cloth around her waist.

Holy hell! It was the blonde woman from the beach, Aileana realized. Someone had beaten her to within an inch of her life. She couldn't believe someone so thrashed would still be on their feet. She removed Aileana's gag and brought the cup of water to her lips.

"What is your name? Tell me where we are. Who is that creature?" Aileana said in a rush of words.

"Mah name is Rhona Fagan. He's nae said his name to me. He told me to call him master," she said through swollen lips. "Yer right aboot him being a creature. I dinnae ken where we are, but this place is an island. It's surrounded by a dense fog which starts aboot twenty feet from the shore."

"You're the woman I saw abducted from the beach in Durness a few weeks ago," Aileana said.

"Aye, are people searching for me? I've talked to others on this island—they're either slaves or wives of the Finfolk." There was a glimmer of hope in her voice.

"They're others here besides us?" Aileana asked.

"Yes, there are a dozen or so. There are human women who've had children with these creatures. The kidnapped humans who are here are used for slaves and spouses of this island's Finfolk creatures."

"I don't know who or what Finfolk are!"

"They're evil shapeshifters, known in folk tales to kidnap humans to use them as slaves or spouses. I had thought they were no more than a myth until I was kidnapped." Her gaze darted from Aileana to the doorway.

"Please untie me. Together we will overpower the creature!"

"Nay, I cannae risk it. I dinnae think I ken take another one of his beatings!" She shook as she said the words.

"When we escape, we can steal a boat and make our way back to the mainland!" Aileana pleaded with the woman.

She started to laugh like a crazy woman and cry at the same time. Aileana thought the woman had lost her mind. "Please try to calm down, we need to keep our wits about us."

Through her tears, Rhona said, "Wits aboot us? We are on a floating island that shifts. It moves where the Finfolk need it to float and is surrounded by a magical fog. No one has left this island alive; not that any of us humans are aware of!" She sobbed.

"Why did the Finman beat you, Rhona?"

"Because I fought him as he brutally beat another woman. After, he beat me because he enjoyed hurting me. Ye need to eat to keep up yer strength. I made a fish stew. Let me feed ye."

After Rhona fed her and gave her a cup of water to drink, Aileana felt somewhat better under the circumstances. She realized she needed to keep her strength up if she was to hope to escape. Rhona left the room, and Aileana started to think about what Rhona told her about the Finman. How he enjoyed seeing her suffer his beating and forced her to be his slave. He was evil with a sadistic bent. He put new meaning to the words Kendrick had said to her in jest on their motorcycle ride in the country. This creature was *"mean, evil, wicked, bad, nasty,"* and she knew she wasn't going to enjoy his sadistic plans for her. She decided to try to take a different tack with the creature.

An hour or so later—it was difficult to gauge how much time had passed, the Finman returned to the room where he held her captive. He strode into the dark space, moving closer to where she was still tied to the bed.

"I need to use the bathroom," she said.

He untied her feet first and then her hands, not saying a word. Aileana rubbed the circulation back into her hands, they felt as if a hive of bees were stinging them. The returning blood to her numb hands made her wince. She braced herself as she lifted herself to a standing position. Her head still felt the effects of the blow to her jaw. It hurt, but she didn't think her jaw was broken.

"Where?" She looked at him.

He pointed to the item in the corner to use as a chamber pot.

"May I have some privacy for a moment, please?"

He started a maniacal laugh which sent chills through her whole body. "Nay!"

She was not going to let him see how bad the lack of privacy affected her. She looked him in his empty, soulless eyes and said, "Fuck you, you piece of shit!"

She then proceeded to use the pot with her audience's full attention. When she stood up, she tried to regain what she had left of her dignity.

He walked over to her and struck her across the mouth, then he grabbed her arm and threw her on the bed. She knew she couldn't feed his sick need to see her beg and plead. She didn't want to feed into his twisted psyche. He stood at the end of the bed and removed the pants and shirt he wore. He gripped his hard shaft and watched her as he stroked himself into a huge erection.

Aileana knew what was likely to happen next, and she would rather face death than have him even lie next to her. She thought if she got him furious enough, he would beat her to death instead, or at the very least unconscious. At that moment, she did what any crazy person would do in such a situation. Aileana started to laugh at him like she was the one possessed by demons from hell. The more she laughed the more enraged the creature became. She noticed the more he became enraged the more his enormous cock deflated.

He needed her fear to keep his dick hard. Well, that wasn't going to happen now that she knew what his psyche kryptonite was. She continued to roar with laughter at this change in her situation. He lunged at her on his bed and started to beat her. She had to wonder how much a body could take before it gave up the ghost of life. It was her last thought before her world went black.

Chapter 22

Kendrick

He thought he would surprise Aileana and see if she was up for a road trip. They would take the Harley over to the small coastal village of Tongue, which was only an hour east of Durness. Kendrick planned for them to have dinner at the Ben Loyal Hotel. They had a wonderful restaurant called The Ben Their website stated they had "Magnificent views of the Kyle of Tongue, Ben Loyal, Ben Hope and the ruin of Castle Varrich," all from the restaurant.

He also wanted them to enjoy one of the rooms at the Ben Loyal Hotel. He thought it would be a pleasant change for them to sightsee a tad the next day before heading back to Durness.

He pulled up to Skye's cottage on the Harley, just as Skye pulled up to the cottage in her car. "Hello, and how are ye doing this wonderful afternoon?" he said.

"I'm doing fine this day, but by the sound of ye, not as well as ye are." She laughed.

"I'd hope to surprise Aileana with an overnight trip to Tongue for dinner and a bit of sightseeing."

"That is a bonnie idea, bhalaich. Let's go inside and ye can surprise her," Skye said.

They walked to the door, and Skye explained the plans she and the other ladies on the committee for the Samhainn festival had made today. They neared the door, and Kendrick became aware of the odor of dark Fae. The door was ajar; he reached out to block Skye from entering her cottage.

"Something is wrong here, there's a stench of dark Fae! Stay here! Let me check the cottage for Aileana."

Skye's frightened eyes met his, and she nodded in agreement. He moved around the front room, and he could smell the stink of Finfolk in the room. It got stronger as he headed toward the small bedroom he knew Aileana stayed in.

Her bed covers were torn from the bed, yet the rest of the room was untouched. Kendrick could identify there had been a Finman in the room; he also perceived Aileana's fear. He raced to the front door to let her grandmother know what he concluded had happened in the room and to Aileana. He assured Skye that he would find her granddaughter and bring her home. As he assured Skye, he also tried to assure himself he would find her. Kendrick needed help if there was going to be any chance of getting her back. He had to get a hold of Duncan and Torin as soon as possible. He placed a call to Duncan. His brother said they would be at the beach within half an hour and ready to go.

Between the three of them, they came up with a plan. It would be extremely risky for everyone, but he was not going to even think of losing Aileana. Now that their life essences had fused, he would be able to track her specific scent. He was sure the Finman had taken her to their fog-shrouded island. They came to the same conclusion that they needed to use a boat to retrieve Aileana.

If it were only them, they would have just gone in their Selkie form, but Aileana would never make it back without a wetsuit. She would suffer from hypothermia. The water temperature off the coast of Scotland was eleven degrees Celsius this time of year. She would only have to be one hour in the water before her body would shut down.

* * * *

The route the Finman had taken was a wild zigzag path across the water. Kendrick's senses kept them on the correct trajectory. The Finman had worked to throw off anyone that might try to follow. Perhaps he didn't realize that Aileana had bonded with a Selkie. He most likely thought it was only sex between a human and Selkie.

They'd been out in the skiff for about three hours. It felt like an eternity to Kendrick thinking about what must be happening to Aileana. It seemed they went in circles, going one way and then the next. Finally, they came upon the blanket of paranormal fog. Duncan was to stay with the skiff as Torin went with Kendrick. They swam to the island as Selkies and transformed on the shore to naked men. No help for being naked; they did what they had to. They left their skins hidden in the crevices of the rocks, which were further up on the shore. The Selkies enchanted their seal skins so no Finfolk would be able to locate or steal them.

There was no light on the island from either the stars or the moon, and no firelight from inside the stone shelters the Finfolk lived in. The Finfolk must have felt secure in the fact that the magical mist would conceal their island home. Kendrick could see a large stone shelter, which reeked of the same stench of the Finman that had been in Skye's cottage. Kendrick could barely distinguish Aileana's honeyed spice scent over the creature's fetid musky stench.

They crept up to the shelter. There were no actual doors on the structure only a large opening. The windows were arrow slits, same as were found in the curtained walls of medieval battlements beneath the crenellations. Kendrick silently made his way into the structure with Torin close behind. There they heard grunting sounds coming from the room to the left of the cold fireplace. They hugged the wall as they eased into the room. There on the bed, tied naked, was an unconscious Aileana. On the other side of the bed was the Finman who'd just kicked a blonde woman who cried out as her body hit the floor.

Kendrick picked up the pitcher that sat on the table next to where he stood and brought it crashing down on the back of the creature's head. He groaned as his body swayed. The creature was only momentarily stunned before he swung around to face Kendrick. His rapid movement from the bed was a surprise as he roared with rage and lunged toward Kendrick. He knocked him to the floor with his momentum. Kendrick punched the Finman in the face and fought to get a few well-placed blows in. They rolled across the stone floor trading blows when Kendrick landed a solid wallop to the creature's jaw. He was able to maneuver behind him to reach around and get him in a chokehold. The Finman struggled as the lack of oxygen rendered him unconscious. Kendrick dropped his body to the floor.

Torin went to the other side of the bed to help the sobbing young woman. He covered the woman with a nearby shawl that lay on the table. While Torin comforted the traumatized blonde woman, Kendrick untied the cords that bound Aileana to the wall and bottom of the bed.

"Torin, can ye manage to calm the woman? If not, use yer magic to render her into a soothing sleep. We will take her also. She is the young woman that was kidnapped from the beach a few weeks ago."

Before Torin could use his magic on the woman she reached the dish with a knife sitting on its edge. She whirled back around to the creature and plunged the knife into the creature's throat to the hilt. The only sound now was the gurgle of the life flowing from the Finman.

"He cannae hurt nay one else now. He was a pure evil creature. He enjoyed inflicting pain, suffering, and humiliation on others. He needed to die," the young woman said with an eerie calmness.

A Selkie's Magic

Torin eased the traumatized woman into a healing slumber, lifted her into his arms and carried her from the stone structure. Kendrick couldn't bring himself to cover Aileana with any item from this place of pain and evil. She was battered and bruised. She had a huge swelling on the side of the face where he had thrashed her. The Finman had also bitten her on the inside of her upper thigh. He could only imagine what had happened to his sweet lass. If the creature wasn't already dead, he would have eviscerated the Finman and left him to die a slow agonizing death for violating his mate in any way. The only thing that mattered now was that Kendrick had her and hoped she would come back to him. He loved her and nothing could ever change his thoughts or feelings about her. He would hope her mind would heal as her body healed. He gently scooped her into his arms and made his way out of the cottage. He followed the downward path to the water's edge to the rocks where Torin and he hid their pelts.

After retrieving his pelt from the rocks, Kendrick lowered Aileana into the near icy water and washed away the last traces of the foul Finman. He wished he could do the same for her mind. He wanted to take away this horrific experience from her memories.

Just off the shore, he met up with Torin who swam with one arm holding the blonde woman's head above the water. Torin had wrapped the blonde woman's body in his pelt to keep her as warm as possible until they reached Duncan and the skiff. Kendrick had done the same with Aileana and his pelt.

His mind signaled to Duncan once the fog had shrouded them. They used their own form of sonar when visual cues were not available. Seals could use echolocation; the Selkies were lucky, in that they are able to use their sonar while in human form. They swam toward the skiff as Duncan moved the boat closer to them in that damn magic-induced fog. At last, they found his brother with the skiff. He helped lift the women into the boat, and they rubbed their limbs with the towels they brought, trying to warm up the women. They laid the women in the bottom of the skiff on a bed of quilts and covered each with blankets.

Kendrick told Torin that when the blonde female woke he needed to scrub her memories for the sake of all Seelies. If the world discovered evidence of Unseelies, the Seelies would become known as well.

It would also be better for the woman to have no memory of what had happened to her. No recall of the island of Hildaland, or that she had killed someone, creature or not. It would be better to have amnesia than to remember her treatment at the hands of the Finman.

Their plan was to get her clothed and drive her to the hospital in the nearby village. To tell the hospital, they found her wandering around and recognized her from the poster the police had put up in Durness. At the hospital, they would be able to treat her injuries from her beatings and whatever else the Finman had inflicted upon her.

The boat came to rest upon the sandy shore of a secluded beach. Duncan and Torin had left the car on the cliff above the beach. They carried the unconscious women up to the car. Kendrick had Duncan drop Aileana and himself off at his cottage. Then he asked Duncan to contact their Selkie healer and have her meet them at his cottage. Kendrick also contacted Skye to let her know they had located Aileana, and she was alive but badly beaten. He told her they were at his cottage and the Selkie healer was on her way to help.

Skye and the healer arrived at the same time. They hurried into the room where Kendrick had placed Aileana.

The healer went to work assessing Aileana's injuries while Skye grabbed a bowl of warm water and a few cloths to wash the blood from her. Her grandmother went to work removing the crusted blood from Aileana's face to see what injuries she suffered. During that time, their healer told Skye and Kendrick that Aileana had been lucky considering how bad it appeared. She had no broken bones, just bruised ribs, along with a couple of somewhat loose molars that would tighten back up in the next week or two. The teeth would be a little tender in the meantime, but she wouldn't lose them. The swelling in her eye would go down in the next week. Skye washed and applied an antibiotic ointment to the bite on her granddaughter's inner thigh and covered it with a bandage.

Kendrick wanted to know the full extent of her injuries. When Skye left the room to get fresh water, he asked the healer if the Finman had raped Aileana.

The healer turned and stared into his eyes. "Prince Kendrick, will it make a difference in how ye feel about the young lass if ye know she has been violated by the Finman?"

He peered into her wise eyes and could answer in full honesty. "Nay, I love her so deeply, I am truly glad she is alive and I was able to bring her home. The whole time I searched for her, I kept thinking I couldn't bear mah life without her in it. I only hope for her sake, she can move past what has happened to her."

"To answer yer question, Prince Kendrick, I am unsure if the Finman violated her or not. There are no vaginal lacerations or tears, and there doesn't appear to be any trauma to the vaginal area. I would say no, he didn't."

"I will do all in mah power to help her move past whatever the Finman has done," he said.

Aileana's grandmother came back with the fresh water and cloths. As she approached the bed where Kendrick sat, Aileana opened her eyes and said through her split lip, "I'm still alive?"

Kendrick gazed down at her bruised and swollen face and said, "You're still with us, *mo luaioh,* my darling."

She gave him a small twisted grin. "That was worse than getting *worked* at *the wedge* and getting a *sand facial* at the same time."

Skye glanced at her and said, "I am thinking that is something that is not too pleasant to experience, aye."

"Fer sure, *Seanmhair*! But I made it out alive, which is *unreal,* for that I am grateful. Kendrick, how did I get here?"

"Because of the bond we share, I was able to track ye across the water to the Finman's island home of Hildaland. Otherwise, I would not have found ye."

"There was also a young woman by the name of Rhona Fagan. He kidnapped Rhona from the beach a few weeks ago. We need to find her."

"Dinna fash, Aileana, we brought her back with us. She's safe now and receiving treatment at a hospital in Scourie," he told her.

"What happened to my captor?"

"After mah fist connected with his jaw, he went down for the count; he was out cold on the floor. The blonde woman grabbed a knife that was on the table and stabbed him through the throat, severing what would be the equivalent of your human carotid artery. He's dead."

"Is Rhona all right? She was so frightened of him and too afraid to escape. I tried to talk her into releasing me and making a run for it."

"There would have been no escape from the island of Hildaland. The island was at least two hours off the coast of Scotland by boat. The magic of the mist that surrounds the island would have kept ye from finding yer way out of the fog."

"Kendrick, the creature was so malicious. He enjoyed seeing the pain he inflicted, and it was as if it was a drug for him. Once I saw that he needed to inflict pain to make himself aroused I shut down my emotions and showed no fear. And I laughed at him as he exposed himself and started jerking himself off to frighten me. I was scared to death! He said he planned to make me his. But I understood if I laughed like a person that belonged in an insane asylum, he would beat me until he killed me. I didn't expect to live."

"Och! You're very brave, little one. Why don't ye rest and regain some strength? I will just be in the other room if ye need me."

"I want to stay here, next to her side. I will just get comfortable in that overstuffed chair ye have in yer bedroom," said Skye.

He nodded to Skye. He understood the terror she had faced today with the real fear of losing her granddaughter.

The Selkie healer said, "I've done what I kin do, she just needs rest and time to heal. Ye know where I will be if ye need me, mah Prince."

He thanked her and walked her to her car. Kendrick went back to the cottage and looked in on Aileana. She was fast asleep, and so was her grandmother. He walked to the overstuffed chair and placed a blanket in Skye's lap. Kendrick moved back to his front room and got comfortable on his old worn couch before the low burning peat fire.

He had to wonder why the Finman had come into a home to snatch a female. It was not their way. Finfolk were generally opportunity kidnappers. For him to lie in wait and go into a home up above the beach was not in character for Finfolk.

Chapter 23

Aileana

What an upside down world Aileana felt she'd dropped into. She had a totally amazing lover who just happened to be a Selkie prince. She'd been kidnapped by a Finman who planned to do horrible things to her. Thank the powers that be, the Finman was now dead and wouldn't hurt any other women. She was thankful Kendrick had been able to find her before it had got any worse for her.

Finding out her father had been a Selkie, but no longer had any memory of being Selkie—yeah right! That sounded like a typical family's everyday drama—yeah right! Not even in Hollyweird did that shit happen.

Kendrick had cued her in on how lucky she was to make it off the mystical island of whatever. They talked about how they would make the village a safer place for all time and not just now. They came up with an idea that might work if they could get the town council to approve the proposal. Best of all, it would not cost the village a dime. The cost of the project would be donated by Kendrick's family.

Their idea happened to be decorative signs posted on the beach and in the village about the historical significance of the village of Durness. Each sign would include a different bit of local history in the signage. At the bottom of the information on Durness would be the sign of the Christian cross. It was true that the Finfolk abhorred the sign of the Christian cross above any other symbol and would stay as far away as possible. The village people didn't need to know that aspect, or why the cross on the signs was present.

A Selkie's Magic

It had been a week since her Finman ordeal; she nearly appeared like herself again. She was just a black and blue bruised version of her old self. Even the bite the Finman took from her inner thigh had scabbed over. On the third day after her rescue, Kendrick brought Aileana back to her grandmother's home. He thought she might heal faster being with her grandmother and being in her own bed. She thought she understood his reasoning. There was a part of her that wondered if he viewed her as damaged goods. Aileana didn't know if she could take him having a change of heart about her. They had discussed little of what happened in the Finman's bedroom on the island of Hildaland. The only thing they discussed in any depth was the signs for the village and beaches. Aileana felt Kendrick avoided the discussion of the island. Was he doing it because he believed it was too raw a wound for her, or was it something he didn't want to know the details of?

The part of her which had the most trouble healing was her mind. It surprised her. She thought she preferred to have him beat her to death rather than for her to submit to the vile creature. Aileana thought she been made of tougher stuff than someone who would give into death. She understood now, as long as she was alive, there was hope and to never give up, at least go down swinging. She realized as soon as she could get over her night terrors and put a little time and distance, it would help with her recovery. At this time, Aileana was still jumpy and afraid of her own shadow. She seemed to have lost the woman she once was, the woman who was fearless and up for any new adventure. She hoped to find that woman again.

It also seemed strange to not discuss the kidnapping with her family or anyone for that matter. The only ones who were aware of her trauma were her seanmhair, Kendrick, and his Selkie clan. She understood why it was so important to keep this confidential; a whole race of beings was at stake.

Kendrick wanted her to meet his brother, Duncan, and their close friend, Torin, who helped with her rescue from the island. He planned to bring them to her *seanmhair's* cottage. Aileana decided to prepare food that was popular back home in Southern California. She chose to make, a Mexican meal. She had prepared to cook up a batch cheese enchiladas, beef tacos, Spanish rice, and refried beans with fresh salsa. She wondered what the guys would think of the meal. Aileana hoped they would enjoy it as much as her friends back home did.

She started thinking about meeting Duncan and Torin. She had nothing but gratitude for them risking their lives for her. She also wondered what they thought of Kendrick hooking up with a human. Aileana hoped the guys received news of how Rhona fared. Rhona's treatment at the hands of the Finman had been so much worse than what she'd endured. Aileana had been his prisoner for less than twenty-four hours, but Rhona had endured enslavement by the creature for over two weeks. She couldn't imagine what she must have endured during her time of captivity.

In her room, she tried to make herself presentable after freshly showering. Her hair dried in soft waves that fell around her face and over her shoulders, hiding a few of the bruises which were starting to fade to yellowish-green. Aileana guessed faded yellow was better than black and blue. She even applied a small amount of her favorite tinted moisturizer, hoping the tint might hide the worst of the bruises. Just a touch of mascara and a hint of her peach-colored lip gloss. Aileana was in her comfy well-worn 501's Levi's, her favorite oversized cream-colored fisherman sweater, and on her feet, her Timberland boots. She was ready, but a tad apprehensive to meet the Selkies who saved her. They had seen her at her most vulnerable.

She'd always thought of herself as tough and a woman who was able to take care of herself. Clearly, in that situation, she wasn't as tough as she believed.

Next thing she knew, she heard a knock on the door. She heard her *seanmhair* let the guys in. Aileana walked into the front room and got her first view of the other two who'd rescued her. Duncan was as gorgeous as Kendrick, but he was carnal in corporeal, it radiated from him.

At first glance, he appeared a bad boy biker. He was tall, six feet four or so, and about two hundred and twenty pounds of pure muscle. He wore his dark hair short and carelessly tousled. The feature which seemed to draw her eye to him was all the black ink on his body, and she was only able to see just so much. Aileana was sure the ink-covered body parts she wasn't able to see. She could see the nipple rings poking beneath his tight black muscle T-shirt. They appeared to match the size of the silver hoops in his pierced ears that seemed to be the size of a quarter. Besides his body art and body piercings, he had the darkest sapphire blue eyes she'd ever seen. Aileana thought, *Oh my God, good thing Adaira is not here.* This hunk of a tatted-up muscle dude was just up her alley when Adaira was in her rebellious, wild girl mode. *Holy mother of Eros! Not good, not good at all, please don't let them run into each other.*

When Aileana finally took her eyes off Kendrick's brother, she smiled over at Torin. Now, Torin was as different as day is to the night next to the Morgan boys. He was blond-haired with a muscular build, about six foot two, with green eyes like Aileana. His hair was what she would call medium length shaggy. Kind of like that character on the TV show *NCIS Los Angeles*, the surfer dude, Marty Deeks. Just like humans, Selkies came in all sizes and all shades of hair color. Her father had the dark auburn hair that her grandmother and she shared.

Aileana glanced at all three of the males in the room. "I just wanted you all to know how much I appreciate what you did for me on the island. I would do anything for each of you. I am in your debt. If ever there's a time you need anything, I'll do anything in my power to help and please, I mean this with my whole heart."

Duncan was the first to say something. He stared her in the eyes and said, "Aye, I will come to ye someday with a favor. Then ye kin repay me." He winked.

Kendrick, she could swear snarled at his brother and said, "Ignore him. He's an arse."

"Well, brother, I may be an arse, but I am a fun arse." Duncan laughed, his own wicked grin in place.

"You're quite the charmer, aren't you?" Aileana chuckled.

Torin replied, "Lass, we were glad we were able to help ye and the other lassie."

"Speaking of Rhona, have you spoken to her since you took her to the hospital?"

"Aye, we paid her a visit a few days ago. She's healing and soon to go home to her family," said Torin.

"How she's dealing with the kidnapping?"

"Och! Didnae Kendrick explain that we used our Selkie magic on her to wipe those memories away?" said Duncan.

"No, I guess he left that detail out of our conversations." She turned to where Kendrick leaned against the fireplace.

"It was better that way, and necessary to erase those memories. We coudnae let her tell anyone about magical creatures the humans dinnae know exist. Plus, would ye want her to remember what she endured at the hands of the Finman?" Kendrick replied.

"What does she think happened to her?" Aileana said.

"The lass doesn't know what happened to her in that two-week period. Only that we found her walking around down on the beach. The doctors did tell her she had been beaten within an inch of her life, but that was all they knew," Kendrick explained.

"Aileana, yer enchiladas are finished. The timer on the oven just went off," her grandmother said.

"I guess it's time you guys try some of my favorite foods. Hope you like Mexican food." She could see by the glances they gave to each other that this possibly wasn't anything they had tried. She laughed. "You'll love it. You haven't lived until you've tried my gnarly Mexican food. It is so sick."

"What are ye talking about, lass? We don't want to be sick on gnarly Mexican food," said Duncan.

Aileana started laughing until her sides were hurting and her eyes watering. "Sick is a term that means impressive. And gnarly is something that is really, really good," she said, still giggling. "Sorry about that, I forgot I am not talking to other surfers."

"Och! I understand now. Ye worried me for a minute." Duncan smiled with a slightly confused expression on his handsome face.

Chapter 24

Kendrick

Aileana and Kendrick made plans to jog along the beach and then go out surfing. They decided to meet on the beach around nine in the morning. Kendrick thought he would surprise her later with something different she would delight in. He wanted this to be a special day of having fun and enjoying each other. She now felt up to exercise. Her ribs still gave her a few twinges when taking deep breaths, but her face was back to its beautiful contours, her lush lips back to their kissable self.

Kendrick only had a couple days before he needed to go back to the oil rig for his next shift of twenty-eight days. He had no idea how he'd be able to tolerate being away from Aileana that long. He still wasn't sure he could get her to commit to being his life mate. Kendrick knew she cared and enjoyed his company, but that was a long way from binding with a life mate. He still needed to discuss with her what it entailed—centuries with a Selkie mate.

Aileana was able to jog the beach for three miles with him with no problem. She then went up to her grandmother's cottage on the cliff to change into her wetsuit and grab her surfboard. As she came down the steps to the beach her face glowed with happiness. The wetsuit showed off the lush curves of her petite frame. Kendrick couldn't control his body, and his cock was in full on arousal mode. She took a glance at him and raised her curved eyebrows in mock disbelief.

"Down, boy!" She laughed.

"See what ye do to me. It's yer fault, not mine," he said with a large grin on his face.

A Selkie's Magic

"Surf now! Play later, dude," she impishly chided him.

She ran into the surf and called back over her shoulder, "Try to keep up, *grommet*, and I will teach what you need to know."

He raced out to the area around the rock pillars; of course, he got there first. Kendrick would be a pretty poor excuse for a Selkie if he couldn't outswim a human. Aileana showed him how to take off and do the pop-up to rise up on the board. He was able to catch some of the waves after a few false starts. Kendrick started to get the hang of her favorite sport. He could see why she enjoyed surfing so much. Plus, the sea just happened to be his preferred place to be.

He decided to share his surprise with her now. Kendrick asked her to wait for him out in the water while he took one last ride into shore. He went to the shore and placed her board on the sand and ran back into the water and swam out to her.

"Why did you leave the board on shore?" she asked.

"I thought ye could use a little fun with yer Mr. Seal," he said.

"You want to have sex out here?"

"That sounds fun, but it's not what I had in mind at this moment." He laughed.

"What did you have in mind?"

"I'm going to put mah pelt on and ye can grab me around mah neck. Then hold on while I take ye for a Selkie swim." He watched her expression change to wonder and curiosity. "I'll be right back. I will go get mah pelt. It's out on the pillars."

"Okay, Mr. Seal, that sounds awesome. I am so ready. Let the fun begin."

He swam to the pillars and climbed up to the area where he kept his pelt, shucked off his swim trunks, and grabbed his Selkie skin. He walked naked around to the front of the rocks to face the beach and dove in holding his pelt. Kendrick entered the water and slipped into his fur skin to become a Selkie seal. He swam over to Aileana. As he approached, she started talking to him.

"Mr. Seal, I knew you were special the first time you swam with me back in August. I just didn't realize how special you were."

She reached out and started to stroke his head, then moving down stroked his back. Aileana reached to hold on around his neck, and she wrapped her legs around his torso. It felt wonderful and strange at the same time. He had never had any human on his back while in his Selkie form. Kendrick started to glide forward, propelled by his large hind flippers. Aileana had latched on to him like a starfish clinging to a rock. He let her get used to swimming on top of the water and then they took a few short dives to see how she liked it. He was able to catch her making happy sounds underwater and decided to dive a little deeper. He didn't stay under more than two minutes to see how Aileana adjusted. Kendrick headed back to the surface. When we reached the surface, he swiveled his head around to gauge her reaction. Her smile said it all. She was enjoying this experience.

"We can stay down longer. I will signal you when I need to come up for some air, okay?"

He let her know he understood by barking once and nodded his head. Kendrick decided to swim with her over to an old shipwreck that was in fairly shallow water. The ship went down in a storm over a hundred and fifty years ago. The humans had not located this wreck, so it was still basically untouched. The only items that had been taken were gold coins from what was left of a chest. The Selkies used the gold as they needed to help their clan. Old shipwrecks were one of the ways the Selkies had of procuring wealth.

They approached the wreck and he could see other Selkies swimming among the rocks. There down below was the ship. They had the attention of all the Selkies now. Kendrick's brother and Torin were the first to swim toward them. They surfaced at the same time Duncan and Torin did.

Aileana glanced at the Selkies and said, "You must be Duncan," to the Selkie that appeared a lot like Kendrick only somewhat larger. She turned to the other Selkie and said, "You must be Torin, with your light pelt."

Kendrick barked at her to let her know she was correct.

"I'm so stoked, Kendrick. This whole experience is so surreal," she said.

He nodded his head and barked again. At the same time, his brother spoke to him using their telepathic ability. *"What are you doing out here with Aileana?"*

Kendrick assured him it was all right that she was here. *"She is mah life mate. I wanted to show her how we live when we are in our Selkie form."*

"So she agreed to be your life mate?"

"Och, I haven't quite got that far yet."

At that Torin, let out a loud bark that could raise the dead.

Torin spoke to his mind and said, *"Sounds like you're worried she won't become your life mate to me."* He made, a rude snorting noise.

Aileana had been stroking Kendrick's sides. She glanced at Duncan and Torin and then back to Kendrick.

"You're communicating with each other! Aren't you?"

Kendrick nodded to her to let her understand she was correct. He also let Duncan and Torin know that their laughter wasn't something he wanted to hear. He let them comprehend he would show them no mercy when they were in the middle of convincing their life mates of the benefits of a Selkie lover.

With that, Duncan's thoughts came across crystal clear. *"Brother, I for one have no intention of settling down to just one female. There are too many human and Selkie females to make happy to just choose one female."* He laughed. *"Ye, as the next heir, need to obtain a life mate."*

The whole time Duncan and he were telepathically linked, he noticed that Torin was quiet. *"Torin, how do ye feel about a life mate?"*

"Kendrick, if I should be so lucky to find a life mate, I would consider myself an extremely fortunate Selkie. Be she human or Selkie, it matters not."

At these words, Duncan's head whipped around to stare at their close friend. Kendrick could tell that Duncan was surprised by Torin's thoughts. With that, they let Kendrick know that they were leaving to start back home.

Kendrick took Aileana down to get a closer view of the old wreck. It was just in about thirty-five feet of water. He was able to get them down quick enough for her to view it up close. After a couple more dives, he decided to call it a day and head back to the pillars that were in front of the cliffs near Skye's cottage.

They approached the rocks from the back. Aileana understood he needed to return to his humanoid form. She let go of his neck and slid off his back.

Kendrick moved over to the rocks and removed the Selkie pelt. He climbed to the area where he always stashed his pelt and grabbed his swim trunks. He put the trunks on, and then dove back into the water and swam over to where she waited for him.

Chapter 25

Aileana

Kendrick asked her to have dinner with him at his cottage. He said was preparing something special for dinner. This would be their last time together before he went back to the oil rig for another twenty-eight-day shift. She thought of all that time they would be apart. She wanted to make tonight extraordinary, and something he would remember while he was out on the rig. She also hoped that it would make it easier for her to be without him for the next month.

She still hadn't the courage to voice how she felt about him. Aileana needed to figure out her emotions toward Kendrick. She started to believe she might be able to trust this male. Kendrick had risked his life to save her from the Finman. She couldn't think about getting hurt again. It would crush her to have Kendrick deceive her. Aileana needed to remember that Kendrick was nothing like her last bad choice in the boyfriend department.

The night was beautiful, clear and crisp, the temperature averaging around forty-five degrees Fahrenheit. The moon was full and lit the night sky. Walking to Kendrick's cottage happened to be an easy stroll, especially with the moon shimmering on the ocean. She was still in a state of astonishment from their afternoon Selkie swim. She couldn't stop thinking how incredible the experience had been. Never in her wildest dreams would she ever have imagined something so amazing could happen, or was even possible.

Aileana soaked in the bathtub, trying to relax her tired muscles. It was a lot harder to hang on to a Selkie or a seal than she would have believed. Kendrick moved so fast through the water, as if jet propelled. His Selkie body was large and thickly muscled. His fur was soft with a dense undercoat. In her thoughts, she still felt the sensation of her fingers deep in his pelt. She'd used her hands to caress his tightly bunched muscles as he thrust through the water. She'd been amazed at the ease with which he had gotten them both down to the shipwreck. She would never have been able to swim to the wreck on her own. She would've needed scuba gear. The speed at which he was able to swim made the difference of not needing an oxygen tank.

She thought about the ways she would be pleasing him tonight as she dressed with seduction in mind. She wore one of the new dresses she'd brought from home. She had purchased a couple of cute dresses from a tiny boutique on Melrose Avenue in Beverly Hills. She chose the short black cashmere sweater dress with the scoop neckline. She didn't know if she would actually be given a chance or a reason to wear them, but she'd thrown the dresses in the suitcase anyway. She sprayed a small amount of her favorite fragrance, Eternity; she loved the mood it put her in. Instead of her usual ponytail, she left her hair down long and loose with the soft curls hitting just above her waist. She wore a pair of black ballet flats to make her walk to easier.

Aileana knocked on the door of Kendrick's cottage. She could hear him inside banging some pots or pans. He must have been in the middle of preparing their meal.

He called out, "Come on in. The door isn't locked."

She let herself in and glanced around the front room. The table was set and the candles glowed around a tiny vase of field flowers. He had a peat fire going in the fireplace. Kendrick's choice of music playing on his iPod through the JBL Stereo Speaker system wasn't soft or romantic, but it was her favorite group. Linkin Park's *Burn it Down* thumped in the background.

Her eyes met his smiling face and she said, "Excellent choice in music, love this group and the song. One of my favorite songs of theirs is *Somewhere I Belong*. The guys in the band are a local group back home; they're from Agoura, CA, which is only about ten minutes from where I live."

She walked over to where he was stirring something on the stove. "What is that delightful aroma?"

"Och! It's my soy butter sauce, for the fresh salmon that's under the broiler. I need to turn it off now before I overcook our fish."

"Wow, I am impressed! Not only are you hot-looking and able to cook, but a Selkie to boot! I would call that a boyfriend trifecta."

"I don't cook often, but I thought it would be enjoyable for just the two of us before I go back out on the oil rig for mah next shift."

"I will miss you while you're away working, but I will stay busy finishing my article for the magazine. Because I've been a bit distracted I am a trifle behind on the piece."

"I will be missing and longing to be with ye as well. Were ye able to come up with a story on the rigs?" he said.

"The story has changed from what I thought I would be writing about. The article is now regarding life on a 'jackup rig' for the men working out at sea."

"How's it going?" he said.

"It is nearly finished. I need to clean it up a tad and then shoot it off to my editor. The men were much more willing to talk about their work and living conditions," she said.

"I've been working for the company now for a few years. I've only run into one man I didn't think was on the up and up. The company must have felt the same way, as they got rid of him soon enough. The company also got rid of the men who killed mah brother, though they had no idea they killed a Selkie, let alone one even existed. The company just thought they were seal killers," Kendrick said.

"At least they had no tolerance for that type of behavior. Shooting seals is definitely wrong."

"Those men just happened to be bad, whether they lived on land or the sea. They ended up paying the ultimate price for their crime."

"Why? What happened to them?"

"After the company fired them from the oil rig, they went to work on a fishing boat. Soon after they began their new job they had an accident. They got tangled in the trolling nets and the deckhands weren't able to cut them loose before they drowned."

"That's horrible! But you know what they say, karma's a bitch," she said.

"Let's not talk about work. Let me tell you how incredible ye look and I love that wonderful fragrance yer wearing. It goes well with yer natural spicy scent," he said.

"Well, thank you, kind sir. My thoughts were along the same lines. I noticed you're so handsome in your black knit sweater and black jeans. The land version of your black as midnight Selkie pelt."

Kendrick moved away from the kitchen and came and took her in his strong arms. She felt the corded muscles of his biceps and forearms as he embraced her. He made her feel so safe and cared for when she was with him. The ice in her heart melted a smidgen every time she was with him and she thought there was a strong possibility she would be able to love again. She wouldn't let her past failed relationship cloud her view of Kendrick. Aileana realized she had strong feelings for Kendrick. She just didn't trust her judgment enough to know if it could be love. *Yeah, like the last time turned out so well. Not.*

"Let's eat before the fish is cold. Besides the salmon, I also made baked potatoes, carrots, and peas. I made just plain food except for the soy butter sauce for the grilled salmon. What is that under your dishcloth that ye brought?"

"I baked a blaeberry and sloe berry crumble. *Seanmhair* had put up a batch of the summer blaeberries. Then after we had our first frost last week, the sloe berries are now ripe and sweet," she said as she lifted the dishcloth to give him a peek at the crumble.

"It sounds delicious and looks tasty. Let's sit down and enjoy our meal," he said as he pulled out her chair from the dining room table.

The meal that Kendrick prepared was fantastic, but more so than the dinner was he wanted to make their time together special. How would anyone not find this male a person of worth? Aileana felt the walls around her heart had begun to crumble.

After their dinner, Kendrick had cleared the table and placed the dishes in the sink when Aileana came up behind him. She wrapped her arms around his waist and laid her head on his back. She inhaled his wonderful, clean, masculine scent, which brought thoughts of his lovemaking skills. She lowered her hands and rubbed the large bulge in the front of his pants. It had the effect on him that she desired. He was rock-hard in seconds and his cock wanted to break free of its confines.

He made that rumbling noise in his throat that only a Scot can make. She unbuttoned his Levi's and reached in and got a hold of his heavy erection. She slid his jeans down below his taut ass so they wouldn't hinder her movements as she grabbed his heavy ball sac and gently massaged him. With her right hand, she caressed his thick long shaft. Aileana's fingers glided up and down in a firm rhythm. Her fingers traveled to touch the velvety smooth tip of his shaft. She glided her fingers against the slit at the head of his cock to coat his erection in his pre-cum. She wanted to make him come where he stood.

She turned him to face her. She wanted him to watch her face and see what he did to her. She touched his sensitive slit, then brought her fingers to her lips and let him observe how much she savored the taste of him. She delighted in his growls of pleasure—they were the sounds she needed to hear. His satisfaction was at the top of her priority list. His dark obsidian eyes devoured every movement she made. Her desire for Kendrick had drenched her panties. She realized his Selkie beast was aware of her arousal, her scent had driven him into a frenzied lust. She could feel her cream would soon be wetting her thighs.

Kendrick started to move his hands to caress her breasts. As much as she wanted his touch, she desired to prolong the need as long as possible.

"You'll have to wait to touch me. I want to take us to a higher level of pleasure. Are you game?"

"Aye, *mo luaioh*, I will be yer willing Selkie male, fur whatever games ye wish to play. I'm sure I will delight in them as well," he said in a husky voice.

"Your Gaelic gets more pronounced the harder you get."

"My brain turns to porridge when yer hands work mah cock like yer're doing now."

"I don't want you to be thinking, I only want you to enjoy what your body experiences as I pleasure you." She slid to her knees in front of her large Selkie lover.

"Dinna fash, *mo chride*, my heart, yer making it…verra hard…and hard to think about anything but what yer sweet mouth's doing to mah cock," he murmured.

She heard him tell her not to worry, he was enjoying and not doing too much thinking at this point in time. Aileana slid her tongue along the large vein on the underside of his pulsating thick shaft. She heard him suck in his breath as she took one of his balls into her mouth, tonguing it as she gently sucked one ball then the other. She was in her own heaven, breathing in his own distinctive intoxicating male scent. She was so aroused that she squirmed with her own need, close to an orgasm without him even touching her. She had to wonder if, in fact, he used his Selkie magic on her.

If it was his magic, she was in a blissed-out state and wanted nothing more than to bring him to his own explosive release. She craved to have him shoot his hot load. She needed to taste and experience all Kendrick could give her. Aileana was on fire for this male and only he could quench this raging inferno inside her before it consumed her.

She could feel the rising tide of his passion as his cock kept jerking with the attention she gave him. His shaft was as hard as the quartzite beyond the breakers. The massive flared head of his cock pulsated with each rapid beat of his heart. She wrapped her arms around his taut hips and gripped his clenched ass cheeks.

"Aileana, I am coming," he said between his gritted teeth.

She let him know that she understood by taking him deeper in her mouth and tugging harder on his thick length. His breaths were now short, quick pants as he reached his climax and roared with his release. Within moments, she had a mouthful of his salty, sweet cum.

Chapter 26

Kendrick

Tonight needed to be special. Kendrick didn't want to think how hard it would be without his bonded life mate for the next four weeks. He needed more time to show her they were truly bonded life mates. He experienced a strong connection when he pulled her from the sea that evening of the storm, two months ago. Kendrick was positive the first time he made love to her, the bond was now unbreakable. He was trying to take the relationship slow and let her come to the same conclusion. Since he understood they were life mates, he would never be happy with anyone else. No one would ever be able to replace Aileana in his life, which was how it worked after a bonding took place. Whereas finding a life mate didn't happen for all Selkies.

He'd finished putting together a special dinner for her. There, beyond the kitchen, the table looked as if Martha Stewart had helped him, he thought. He had the sound system cranking out alternative metal tunes. He realized it wasn't what anyone would call mood music. Consequently, his mood was wild like his Selkie beast, which wanted to take control. He could always cue different music on the iPod when his woman arrived.

The sound of a knock on the door alerted him she'd arrived. With a fumble of the pan, which he almost dropped, Kendrick managed to save the baked potatoes he'd just removed from the oven. *What the hell?* He was as anxious as some untried teen boy. Kendrick needed this woman, and she still hadn't let him know how she felt, other than she had feelings, but wasn't sure if it was love or lust.

He understood she enjoyed their lovemaking, and he, in turn, was consumed with the need to have sex with her. Those feelings went way beyond the desire for sex. He craved her in his life, he had to have her as his mate. Kendrick would marry her in the human tradition and in the Selkie manner of bonded life mates. His animal side wanted to be able to create a new life in her body, after all, it was the Selkie way. He wanted the type of life his parents experienced and the children that went with such a life.

He called out that the door was open and to come on in. What a vision Aileana was in her short, fitted black dress which showed every delicious curve on her sweet body. Her hair flowed down to her tiny waist in an undulating mass of burnished auburn curls. Underneath, his little tomboy lover's veneer was the soul of a sea siren. Subsequently, that sea siren had this Selkie tied in knots. Kendrick was so ready to enjoy all her womanly charms, but there was much more at stake than just enjoying each other's bodies. Consequently, if he played his cards right, he would be able to enjoy all her charms for hundreds of years.

He observed her as she glanced around the front room. He noticed how her large emerald-colored eyes took in the fire burning in the hearth and moved on to the candles that cast a warm glow on the dining table. He could only hope that his intended seduction was having the effect on her that he desired and craved.

He had to control his inner animal just a tad longer; all it wanted was to pounce on Aileana. The old saying was "discretion is the better part of valor," or as Aileana would say, "Whatever." He laughed to himself at the thought. Kendrick was looking at the endgame in this relationship. He could only hope that she was looking at this as a forever relationship and not some time filler.

It turned out they shared similar taste in their music. She commented on the group playing on the iPod as her favorite and gave him a little history of the band. She also checked out the meal he'd prepared and made some mention of his cooking skills. They talked about her work and how it was progressing. She mentioned the article she was writing, and he brought up the topic of what happened to his older brother. A topic which he especially didn't talk too much about—even after all this time it was still a painful subject.

Kendrick let her know his next shift on the rig was going to a long, lonely one for him, one he wasn't looking forward to. Especially since she had no idea how difficult it was for bonded life mates to be away from each other. She would soon understand all too well.

The considerate lover in him took her and held her while he was arguing with his Selkie-self to behave and not scare this woman off.

So instead of pouncing on her, he said, "Let's eat before our fish gets cold."

He thought the comment lame most definitely, but he needed to slow things down and get his mind off her curvaceous body and regain some of his own self-control. He needed to conquer one obsession at a time.

After they finished her blaeberry and sloe berry crumble, she surprised him while he placed the dishes in the sink. He felt the warmth of her body as she placed her arms around him from behind. She lowered her hands to the bulge he sported at the front of his pants, which he'd tried to conceal from her all night.

She lowered his Levi's and gripped his cock with one hand, and in the other, she massaged his ball sac. He was in heaven as she rubbed the pre-cum with her fingers making his cock slick with his own fluid as she played with the slit at the head of his shaft.

When she turned him around to face her, her eyes had an untamed gaze. She had a wild beast in her soul as much as he did. After all, she was her father's daughter; her Selkie side just hadn't been released when she reached the age of the change.

He saw in her eyes, she wanted him as much as he wanted her. Aileana hadn't come to the realization quite yet that it is a need, not just something she wanted. Kendrick was aware of her arousal; he was able to catch traces of the honey-spiced fragrance of her core. As well as sensing the releases of her hot fluids getting her ready for his anticipated entry.

He needn't have worried about his inner beast, she had unleashed him and herself. His little sea siren enjoyed a few games of her own. He was the fortunate recipient and willing playmate of all she was willing to share. He had an extremely attractive woman on her knees in front of him with her lush lips wrapped around his swollen shaft. Her mouth was a marvel, of which he was the lucky recipient. With a passion that only someone who cared can give, she had him at the edge of his sanity as she licked his cock and caressed him to his explosive release.

She sucked his dick dry and swallowed every drop of his cum. It took Kendrick a few minutes to come back down to earth and be able to reciprocate the pleasure her mouth had given him. He reached down, pulled her into his arms, and kissed her sweet mouth. He tasted his own cum on her lips as his tongue probed her lush mouth. Kendrick needed to taste her sweet, honey-spiced, core for himself. He cupped her tight arse in the palms of his hands and let her slide against his erection that just wouldn't stay down. His body blazed, and the only thing which could quench his inferno was Aileana and the moist, delicate folds of her swollen sex.

He gazed into the depths of those large emerald eyes and knew with complete certainty he would only continue to fall deeper under the spell of her magic. It seemed his little human possessed her own enchantment, and moreover, it seemed Selkies were not the only creatures with magic. His gaze slid down her body as his hands reached the bottom of her dress and pulled it up to her waist. He lowered his body until his mouth reached her damp panties. His teeth skimmed the black lace on the side of her thong and lightly grabbed the flimsy lace and pulled until they dropped in a small puddle of silky black lace at her feet.

She ran her fingers through his hair and massaged his head as she enjoyed his attention. Kendrick moved his face back up to her sex and inhaled her sweet scent and nipped at her lush mons. As he nipped her, she let out a gasp and pulled his face in tight to the V between her legs. He gripped her around her slim waist and lifted her to sit on the kitchen counter top. His mouth and lips slowly worked their way up her legs, licking and tasting every inch of his sweet woman. He placed her beautiful firm legs over his shoulders and slid her soft, sweet arse close to the edge of the counter.

He was right where he wanted to be, right between those beautiful legs at her wet glistening pussy. Kendrick placed his hand on her collarbone and eased her back down; she reclined and her lush pussy was right before his face. He rubbed his thumbs over the soft folds of beautiful moist flesh. Her clitoris was engorged with her arousal; he used a thumb to push back on the hood to expose it to his tongue.

His tongue explored the outside and inner folds of her pussy with broad flat strokes. Her moans of pleasure were a magical melody to him. Kendrick took his time and licked in slow, steady circles around her clit. Next, his stiffened tongue probed with fast, firm strokes inside her cream-filled pussy. He had to use one of his hands to hold her down against the counter to keep her from bucking away from his mouth. He felt her passion rise as the tension in her legs and body intensified.

She screamed, "Kendrick, don't stop. I'm so close, I'm almost there!"

"Dinna fash, I'll make sure ye get there," he murmured from the tasty apex between her legs.

He licked his middle finger and moved it inside her pussy to find her delicate ridges. He also used his little finger to toy with the tight rosebud of her arse. At last, he sucked her clit into his mouth with his lips; he sucked and pulled on her swollen bud as his tongue gave her a sweet lashing. Her delicious, fragrant juices flowed down his hand as he continued to pleasure her until she screamed in gratification as she shattered against his mouth and he felt her internal spasms squeeze the finger still inside her. He slowed down his strokes with his tongue and fingers; he eased her through the contractions as he relished each and every one.

Kendrick sensed the tension fade from her body as she came down from the euphoric high of her passion.

"Holy mother of Eros, that orgasm was the most intense orgasm I've ever had!"

"Glad ye found it to yer liking as I plan to continue to give them to ye tonight and for a long time in our future." He smiled at her.

She glanced at him with a saucy tilt to her head and said, "Dude, you better make sure you can back up those promises!"

"Och! Dinna fash, *mo luaioh*, I will never lie to ye," he said with a wicked gleam in his eye.

He reached over to her, pulled her to him and hoisted her over his shoulder. She protested and laughed at the same time.

"Ye ken I cannae take yer protest seriously if ye continue to laugh. Aileana, we've now enjoyed our dinner snack and it's time for our main course," he told her as he carried her to his bedroom.

Kendrick threw her onto the bed and leaped on top of her, straddling her hips. She kept up her giggles as he pulled her soft sweater dress over her head and unfastened the black lace bra.

"Aileana, ye need to stop yer laughter, ye understand the main course is serious business." He proceeded to waggle his eyebrows at her, which sent Aileana into a new fit of giggles.

He removed his shirt and lowered his mouth to latch on to her large pale pink nipple, which thrust out hard and erect from her full breast. This elicited a moan instead of a giggle; her eyes started to dilate as her passion set her on edge. Kendrick tugged on her full globes and moved his hand lower to her wet sex. He could feel her body vibrate and hum with her need. He reached for his rigid shaft and rubbed her wet pussy with the head of his cock. She raised her hips to try and take more of him inside herself; he only let her feel the head slide inside. She begged to be filled now, and he reached for her and flipped her over on her stomach.

Kendrick pulled her to her knees and pushed her head down on the mattress. He positioned his cock at her glistening slit, and in one forceful thrust, he was buried to his balls deep inside the woman he craved more than anything else. On his knees, behind her, he grabbed her breast and squeezed as he thrust in rhythmic strokes of deep penetration inside her body. Their lovemaking drove him wild—the more he heard her moans of ecstasy, the further his beast pushed to take over.

Kendrick lowered his right hand to stroke her clit and tapped her swollen nub. She rocked back and forth on his cock with her own rhythmic movements. When he felt her pussy clench around his shaft his Selkie side demanded him to mark Aileana and make her his. His lips went the slender column of her neck and lavished kisses all the way down. His mouth glided down her neck to where it met her shoulder, right to the area he wanted to mark his woman. There he struck and bit as her orgasm hit, but he didn't break her skin this time, he needed to wait. The power of her orgasm milked him into his own release.

They continued to worship each other's body throughout the night with brief periods of sleep. He felt a quiet desperation in their sex. It was unsaid, but they tried to sate a need for each other that would have to last until they were able to see each other next month.

With dawn's approach came the light of the rising sun on the distant horizon. He needed to let his little human female know just how he felt about her before he went back out on the rig. He needed to know that she would still be there when he finished his month out at sea. He wanted to believe that she trusted him to not hurt her or her heart in any way. They had already been through so much together. His mind kept repeating the same word, *mine!*

She must have felt his eyes on her for she smiled as her eyes opened. Her smile lit up his soul and started the beating of his heart like a trip hammer.

"Morning, sunshine," she said with a satisfied grin.

"Ye are mah sunshine, Aileana," he whispered in her ear.

"You make me happy also, Kendrick," she said.

"Aileana. *Mo chride, tha gaol agam ort.*"

"I am sorry, Kendrick, I didn't understand what you said." There was confusion in her eyes and her brow crinkled.

"What I said, Aileana, is, 'Mah beloved, I love ye.' I know that yer're not ready, and I don't expect anything from ye. But I needed to let ye know how I feel, and I want to make ye mine. Ye dinna have to say anything now, just think about it while I am away for the next month. Okay?"

She reached over and cupped his face in her hands. She then pulled him down to her lips, and they had scorching passionate sex one more time before he had to leave to catch the helicopter to the rig. He longed for her words, but passion would have to hold him over until the next time they could be together.

Chapter 27

Aileana

To see Kendrick leave this morning was much harder than she imagined it would be. To say they'd grown close would be an understatement. However, they arranged to Skype each other on his downtime. It had to be enough for the time being, they had no other options.

She felt so confused about what was going on with her feeling on their relationship. She wanted to say the three little but important words to him. Aileana just wasn't able to get the words to leave her lips. She knew in her heart Kendrick was nothing like the men in her past.

Her history with men was poor. She'd fallen so fast for the wrong type of men, and now that she was with a male of worth, her heart was guarded. *What in the holy mother of Eros did he mean "make ye mine?"* Was she hoping he meant to be together, as in a committed relationship? He spoke of them as bonded and life mates. He said his brain turned to porridge when they were having sex; well hers appeared to turn to mush when she tried to think about being in love with Mr. Seal, Selkie, *whatever.*

From what Kendrick told her of Selkies, it would appear that Meghan Trainor's song, *All About That Bass* seemed to fit most circumstances. As her song said, it was all about some "booty," as in getting some ass for most Selkies. Even Kendrick acknowledged that Selkies were known to have many human lovers, but seldom took a human as a life mate. Was she going to be fighting off her jealous inclinations because other females would be drawn to Kendrick's Selkie beauty? She knew it was her own insecurities triggering the jealousy. But someone in her past had stomped on her heart, and it was awfully hard to trust again. Trust is especially hard to give; especially if one had feelings for a creature known to have the catnip effect on humans.

She thought she'd have plenty of time in the next month to think about her feelings in regards to her Selkie. She needed to finish up the article and get it off to her editor, figuring she would be able to get it done by tonight and email the article in the morning. She'd thought of writing her next article about the sea life off the Scottish coast. Since their salmon dinner last evening, she thought she would do a piece about the commercial salmon farming that began in Scotland in 1969. She'd read in 2002, over 145,000 metric tons of farmed Atlantic salmon was produced. She thought a salmon farming article would be of interest to quite a few people.

She needed to make a phone call to her sister Adaira. Aileana had emailed Adaira and mention she wanted to talk. She would place the call at six p.m. tonight, which would make it ten a.m. Los Angeles time. Adaira said she would be available at ten in the morning her time, and it would work for her now that her Mr. Seal wasn't around to distract her.

All day she'd been looking forward to the time to talk to Adaira, or as their family and friends sometimes called her, Dare. Namely, they had a lot to catch up on. When it was nearly six there, she got all comfy on the couch and ready to catch up with the news on her family. She wondered what they had been up to since she left the California, and she wanted to talk with her sister about the new *man* in her life.

Adaira picked up the phone on the second ring. "Hey, Aileana, it's so good to hear from you! I've missed you."

"Dare, I've missed you, too. What's happening on the Pacific coast? How are you and the family hanging?"

A Selkie's Magic

"We're all doing great, so enough about us. So how's *Seanmhair* doing, and have you met any yummy dudes?" She said it all in a rush.

"Cool your jets and I will tell you everything. *Seanmhair* is doing wonderfully." She laughed.

"Well! I can tell by your tone something is going on out there."

"Yes, Dare, I met someone…kind of."

"What do you mean kind of?"

"Well, I don't know if you remember when I was fourteen, I met a guy named Kendrick when we were visiting Scotland for the summer?"

"That doesn't ring a bell. Wait! Wait a minute. Are you talking about the older, college-aged dude who gave you the pink pearl?" she replied.

"Yeah, he is older than me." As she thought *Yeah, he is a lot older than even Seanmhair, but Adaira doesn't need to know that detail.* "We kind of bumped into each other at the pub," she explained to Adaira, who certainly didn't need to know about her swimming with Mr. Seal, she thought.

"Well, possibly I will have time to meet him if you're still seeing him; I'll be flying out to Scotland after the first of the New Year,"

"It will be wonderful to have you out here, what brings you out to Scotland?"

"I don't want to jinx it, but a job I hope to get. I will tell you more when I arrive."

"I'll keep my fingers crossed for you and your job."

"I fly out for a visit after the New Year, no matter what happens. However, I have some fun plans set up for the two weeks before the end of the year." The excitement was evident in Adaira's voice.

"What's going on in SoCal?"

"Well, for starters, one of my friends has the use of her parents' home on the beach in Playa Del Rey. Her parents are on location in Canada for two months, so it's party time. Her father starts filming some creature feature. Then after a week at the beach, all of us girls are going to Las Vegas for the big blowout on New Year's Eve. Then a few days later I fly out to Glasgow and then drive on up to Durness."

"Wow, you're cramming in a lot in a short time, but it sounds fun. Are you getting a car to drive up to Durness?" Aileana asked.

"The job I hope to be starting said someone will be available to drive me up north. I will go to a final interview close to Durness. I have been online with the company; this will be the face-to-face meeting."

"I'll keep my fingers crossed for you, and I can't wait to have you fill me in on the job!"

"Thanks, Aileana, I can't wait to visit with you and have you fill me in on Mr.Wonderful. Take care and see you soon. Love you."

"Love you too, bye."

Oh, shoot, I forgot to ask about Mom and Dad! I will have to call them later. When Seanmhair is not busy, that way she will be able to talk to Dad and they can get some visiting done over the phone.

Finally, she got the article finished and sent to her editor. He seemed pleased with the piece and said he looked forward to the next article on the salmon industry in Scotland. Now that she had talked to her sister, she wondered what type of job she was interviewing for up in this area of Scotland. She had her degree in geology. She had taken a course over the summer, but hadn't wanted to tell her about until after she finished them. Aileana had no idea if they were related to her geology degree, or if it was some fun course that had to do with her love of photography. She guessed she would find out once Adaira came out for her interview.

She couldn't wait for that evening to Skype with Kendrick. She wanted to let him know the news that her sister would be in Scotland at the start of the New Year. Adaira had remembered who Kendrick was from the past, but they had never met in person. She wanted them to meet and get to know each other. Kendrick was important, and she wanted her sister to see why she was crazy about him.

* * * *

All too slow the time had dragged by. It had only been three weeks since Kendrick had gone back to the rig. She thought for the tenth time that day, *Holy Eros, this has turned into the longest three weeks ever!* They'd Skyped each other when he was off his work shift. The video chats were the next best alternative to actually being in his arms. She would hate to think of not being able to see his handsome face. Even on the video calls, she could view those soulful eyes, and his sinful grin, and it helped with her loneliness, somewhat. Part of her melted inside with each call. She tried not to let him observe just how needy she felt without him. She swore to herself that he must be using his Selkie magic on her; it couldn't be normal to fixate on someone this much. Besides being the most handsome man she'd ever met, he kept her laughing with his wicked sense of humor.

His stories of his and Duncan's pranks on each other were just too hilarious. Kendrick always seemed to have some interesting tale to share with her. Aileana loved hearing about their childhood and the trouble they gave their parents. Kendrick must have been a handful, but the stories he told about Duncan made Kendrick sound like a saint. She was sure Kendrick and Duncan's mother would say something like her mom would say. Her mother often told Adaira and Aileana, "You both gave me every gray hair on my head." *Yeah right!* As if their mom would ever be seen with a gray hair; so, in essence, they truthfully never believed her.

There were four more days until Kendrick got off the rig. She kept sensing a feeling something wasn't right. Every time she talked to him things were going well with his work. But she had an eerie feeling or premonition about something. She had always had premonitions off and on since she was a child. It came as feelings that something wasn't right. The forewarnings were never specific, in turn, just vague feelings that got stronger as time got closer to an event. As her mother would say, it was a "gut feeling." Unfortunately for her, her "gut" didn't work so well on her own personal relationships. Like when she needed to bail on some dirtbag she'd dated, she guessed it was like the old saying: love is blind. Not that she felt Kendrick wasn't true to his word. This sensation was something else she couldn't put a finger on.

Chapter 28

Kendrick

Damn. He counted down the days like never before. Since Aileana had come back into his life, it was harder than hell to be away from her. Duncan had been trying to keep him occupied with his crazy antics on their downtime. It had helped some, but the bond was so strong that she was always in his head. His body was in agony wanting her. He could feel her thoughts, even all the way out on the drilling platform. She still fought the pull her body and mind had with his; she couldn't understand the demand for what it was. He could feel her need for him. The Selkie magic of their joining was too strong for either of them to fight.

Duncan met up with Kendrick for supper. They grabbed a table and sat down to their meal, and the conversation turned to Duncan's plans for his time off at the end of the week.

"So, Duncan, what plans do ye have for yer holiday?"

"One of my friends, which I met on a motorcycle tour of California on Route 1, the Pacific Coast Highway last year, invited me to spend the month at his beach home. I will also have the use of his Harleys. His business has taken him out of the country. I couldn't pass up such a sweet deal."

"That is a sweet deal! How did ye manage to fall into that?"

"Mutual love of Harleys and the road cemented the friendship, and a love of partying and fast women didnae hurt either. Especially since I also promised him the use of mah cottage and bike if he made it over to Scotland." He laughed.

"Not too bad a deal."

"Truthfully, it would have been better if he'd been in town. The man is a party animal. He said he would leave a list of spots I should hit up," Duncan said.

"If I hadn't reconnected with Aileana, I would have been up for a trip. Now I cannae wait until we're in the same room again." He chuckled.

"Damn, bro, ye got it bad!" Duncan laughed.

"Laugh all ye want, Duncan, it will happen to ye someday," he said with a grin.

"Not me, I just want to ride them hard and move on to the next beautiful woman. This way I will see what the Pacific coast has to offer in the way of hot women. Ye know what they say about California girls…And I'll have a change of scenery far from Scotland."

"So it will only be ye going to California?" Kendrick asked.

"Nay, I convinced Torin to join me on the trip. Torin and I plan to tear up the town! We will hit as many nightclubs as possible."

"At least Torin will be someone to try and keep ye from getting into too much trouble. What area of California is yer friend's home?"

"It's on the beach in an area call Venice. The name of the street is called Ocean Front Walk. I don't think I could get any closer to the water. Jim, mah friend, that owns the house emailed me some pictures of the house. It is a huge multilevel bachelor's wet dream," he said with a gleam in his eye.

"When do ye leave for this slice of heaven?" Kendrick laughed.

"I fly out the Monday after we get off the rig. I just need to throw my clothes in a duffel bag, cash my paycheck, and pack mah passport—done!" He grinned.

His brother was a total horn dog as Aileana would say; he could just imagine what kind of trouble he would get into. Thinking along those lines, he didn't think he should mention Duncan's travel plans to Aileana. She would tell him, since her family lived in Southern California, that Duncan should drop by, and introduce himself. That would not be a good idea at all, seeing as Aileana had an unattached younger sister at home.

He knew Duncan had one thing on his mind, and it involved nothing in the way of playing polite with the fairer sex. Duncan was known for a great deal of fooling around, of the hot and nasty variety. Kendrick didn't want to be aiding and abetting anyone's broken heart. Duncan had left plenty of women with broken hearts along his path of debauchery. Kendrick didn't want one of those devastated hearts to be Aileana's younger sister.

This was his last work shift before he was off the rig for the next month. Kendrick wanted to plan something special for Boxing Day with Aileana. This would be her first Yule in the Scottish Highlands. She had experienced plenty of summers in the Highlands but never a holiday after August. Their short days in the winter made it perfect for each and every one of the indoor games he planned to enjoy with her. In the Highlands, they only averaged seven hours of daylight in December, which he was sure made for lots of Scottish births in September.

When they spoke last evening, Aileana invited him to her grandmother's home for Yule dinner. It would be a treat to have Yule dinner at Skye's cottage. Skye was known in the village as one of the best cooks and bakers the village had.

Kendrick was still was thinking about the gift he planned to purchase for Aileana and was also busy making her a special gift of carved walnut. He'd decided on carving a gift that held a special meaning to both of them. It was a carving of a seal with a woman leaning against its body. The woman head was resting on the seal's neck with her long hair splayed across the body.

At the start of his last shift for the month, he met Duncan on the drilling platform. Overnight, the weather changed and they were at the start of a storm. The sky looked dark and angry with the promise of the worst to come.

Kendrick's work assignment was to direct the crane operator with the off-loading of containers from the supply vessel to the drilling rig. Significant swells were causing various problems for the supply vessel, which made it harder for the vessel to get close enough to the rig. The captain of the vessel wanted to give it a try before the weather took a turn for the worst.

Rodric, the crane operator, gave the signal he was ready. The crane turned and came around to extend out over the drilling platform. Rodric then extended the boom out over the sea, lining up the boom perpendicular to the supply vessel. If anyone could make this difficult task happen smoothly, it was Rodric. He had over ten years as the crane operator on offshore rigs. He had a steady hand and an accurate eye for loading and off-loading. Rodric was a mountain of a man, with a good heart and a quick wit, someone Kendrick admired and called a friend.

The wind whipped the rain down so hard it felt like needles as it hit Kendrick's skin. They were practically finished transferring the containers. They only had two more containers to off-load and they would be done. The container hanging from the crane started to move erratically on its path to the rig.

"Rodric, what's going on up there?' Kendrick spoke into the radio he held. "Rodric, come in!" There was no answer on the other end of the communication line. The crate was coming down fast—too fast. It swung in an uncontrolled arc. Kendrick was nearly out of the path of the swinging container when it caught him sideways and slammed him into the platform substructure. He just missed getting smashed between two of the containers, but his head bounced off the steel post. Kendrick saw a blast of light before he lost consciousness.

The next thing he realized, he lay in a hospital bed on shore. The first face he saw was Aileana's. Her eyes were puffy and she seemed beat. Her clothes appeared rumpled and her hair was twisted into a haphazard knot on top of her head. She became aware of him watching her and presented him a smile that lit up the room.

"This is not how I planned our first time together in a month," he croaked. His mouth and throat were parched. "But it is a pleasant way waking to yer beautiful face." Kendrick tried to reach the tray table near the bed for the glass of water with a straw. He grimaced as his shoulder and back protested the movement.

"Here, let me get that for you. Try not to move around too much." He took a few swallows of the cool water, which soothed his dry throat.

"What happened and how long have I been here?" he asked.

"You've been in the hospital two days now. From what Duncan told me, you were slammed up against a part of the platform structure. You were nearly crushed when the container that was being transferred from the supply ship started to fall, swung wide and caught you."

"I remember trying to raise Rodric on the com line, but he didn't answer."

"Rodric had a heart attack and passed out at the controls."

"Is…is he all right?" he asked, afraid to know.

"They were able to get the medic to him in time to save him. They had to restart his heart. He's already received heart surgery to fix a blocked artery."

In walked Duncan and he came over to the side of the bed.

"Hey, bro, I always said yer're hard-headed, this just proves mah point. Glad to see ye proved me correct." He laughed.

"Glad I kin keep ye amused, Duncan," he said with a smile.

"Well, I'll let you boys catch up, I'm leaving. I think I will go on home, take a shower and catch a nap. Kendrick, I will be back tonight. Duncan, play nice with your older brother, okay?"

Aileana gave Kendrick a quick kiss that promised more to come later when they didn't have an annoying brother watching.

"Duncan, thanks fur being here fur me."

"I haven't left since they brought ye in. But I had to wait to catch the helicopter that brought the men off their rotation. I told *Màthair* and *Athair* aboot the accident. They were relieved to hear ye would be all right, and I was at the hospital with ye," he told Kendrick as he settled into the chair next to the bed.

"Were ye able to clear mah locker out and bring mah duffel bag back?"

"Yes, I had time since I had to wait for the next ride off the platform. I saw the wood carving yer're working on. It's going to be spectacular when yer're finished. Besides a familiar looking seal, the woman appears an awful lot like a certain fiery redhead ye have been keeping company with." He chuckled.

"Has the doctor said how long I have to stay?"

"Ye only have to stay twenty-four hours after you regain consciousness so this time tomorrow yer're free.

Since yer on the mend, I will go check on Rodric and see how he's feeling. He will be glad to hear yer awake and doing much better. Then, I will remake my airline reservation and get myself some California sunshine and wild women."

"Thanks, Duncan, fur, everything, I hope I didn't screw-up yer plans too much."

"Everything is good, just a couple days different on the arrival date. I know ye would be there for me if I needed ye. I will see ye next month back on the rig." As he headed out the door of Kendrick's room, he turned and said, "I have a lot of lassies to make happy in California."

The next day he spoke with his parents over the phone to assure them his brains were still in working order. The headache wasn't too bad and the soreness in his body had started to fade. Thank the powers that be for the Selkies' ability to heal quickly. That was a close call, and he was damn lucky not to have been killed or crippled. There would be no coming back from death or a crippling injury, Selkie magic or not.

He needed to get out of this hospital. Kendrick didn't want to spend a moment more of his time off without Aileana. He needed to accomplish quite a lot before Yule. He had big plans and high hopes for making that stubborn woman his.

He could have made her his so much easier by using Selkie magic, but he didn't want to use magic on the woman he knew was his life mate. He didn't want to wonder for the rest of his life if Aileana only became his life mate because of the magic. He needed her to come to him on her own, and only under the power of their love for each other. If she could come to that conclusion on her own, perhaps she needed a wee bit more incentive to be his life mate.

Chapter 29

Aileana

Kendrick's accident out on oil platform put everything into perspective for her. You can't take any person for granted in your life; a loved one can be taken away in a heartbeat. As the old adage goes "only death and taxes are guaranteed." To think she nearly lost one of the most important people in her life was a wake-up call for her. She would've had a lifetime of regret if something happened to him, and she hadn't even expressed how much she cherished him. Therefore, it was time for her to put on her big girl panties and lay out her feelings to him.

Life was full of risks, and if you didn't make the big moves, you never reaped the big rewards. Trust was a major issue for her. Trust went both ways and Kendrick had entrusted her with his Selkie secret. Now, she needed to trust her instincts that he would take care of her heart.

After getting back from the hospital that night, Aileana made plans with Kendrick to pick him up the next afternoon after the doctor released him. She already had thoughts about what wicked things she wanted to do to him. It had been a long month without his hot, passionate ways. She never thought of herself as being as sexually driven as most of her friends. But since being with Kendrick, she realized she just hadn't been with the right male. Now sex and his hot sculpted body were constantly on her mind.

After the drive home from the hospital, Kendrick was in a playful mood. She surprised him with a Christmas tree, all decked out with ornaments, some of which she had made. It was a sea-themed tree. The tree sparkled with white lights, and brilliant sea blue colored glass ball ornaments which she purchased. She also collected shells from the beach, to which she added clear glitter. She had drilled a small hole in each and hung them with blue ribbon. For the top of the tree, she'd made a large fluffy bow with wide blue ribbon. It was a modest tree, but it brought the mood of Christmas spirit to his seaside cottage.

She also prepared a scrumptious dinner to celebrate his homecoming. They would feast on chicken Parmesan, salad, sourdough rolls, and lots of dry red wine. She decided that their dessert would be each other.

As they walked through the front door of the cottage, he smiled and turned to face her. He wrapped his warm muscled arms around her. Kendrick placed a passionate kiss on her lips and told her how much she meant to him.

"Aileana, the Christmas tree looks perfect. It gives the room an aura of being part of the sea. It's a thoughtful gesture."

"I wanted this to be a fun Christmas, and I loved decorating the tree. This is also my first Christmas away from my mom, dad, and my sister. Besides, the best part is it's my first Christmas with you."

"This is an excellent time to start new traditions of our own," he said with a wicked smile.

"Okay, Mr. Selkie, what new traditions did you have in mind?"

"I have all kinds of mean, evil, wicked, bad, nasty things. Would ye like me to show ye?" He grinned.

"Why, Mr. Selkie, I had hoped you would be up for some reindeer games!" She squealed as Kendrick scooped her up in his arms.

"Forget the damn reindeer; we're going to be playing Selkie games! They invented bedroom games," he murmured in her ear.

Aileana wrapped her arms around his neck and leaned toward him to breathe in his warm spicy scent. His intoxicating scent drew her in like a moth to his flame. The heat between their bodies scorched her. She needed to shed these clothes which were in her way from touching skin to his skin. She couldn't fight her heart any longer; she craved this male in her life. Her brain was now on the same page as her heart.

She enjoyed the salty taste of his skin. As she ran her tongue up his neck to his ear, it only made her think of his other salty, sweet tasting body part she wanted to wrap her lips around. She felt the rumble deep in his chest as he moaned when she nipped his earlobe.

"Kendrick, I need to feel your rigid throbbing length inside of me," she murmured in his ear as he made his way to the bedroom. Her panties were drenched from thoughts of his hard body pushing into her. A deep growl filled the room as she voiced her desires and what she needed from him.

"Woman, *mo chride*, do ye ken what you're doing to me?"

"I have a decent idea if you're experiencing anything like I am," she said with mischief in her voice.

He put her on her feet so close to the bed that the back of her legs brushed against the edge. He wrapped her in the warmth of his arms. Aileana felt his desire rolling off him like the waves in the sea. Her heart pounded beneath her breast. He placed his lips on hers; his kiss was long and slow and she opened to him as the petals of a flower unfolded in the sun. His chest was ripped with solid muscles that she caressed as she slipped her hands beneath his shirt. She lowered her eyes to the huge bulge in the front of his pants, which was just a few buttons away from being in her grasp. The air in the room was charged with a palpable volatile energy.

His dark eyes seemed to glow with a burning fire of his desire as he pulled her sweater over her head and tossed it into a corner of the room. His strong hands palmed her breasts. The pleasurable scrape of his callused hands made her body tingle as they brushed against her pebbled nipples. Aileana moaned with need. Every nerve in her body hummed with sweet anticipation. He brought his mouth down to one of her lace-covered nipples, which brought on a sweet flood of juices that soaked her panties. The fire between them was so intense that she expected to see flames scorching anything within ten feet. Never before had she felt such a sexual intensity.

His inner beast was unleashed and roared to be sated. Aileana's insides clenched with need. She needed to be possessed by her Selkie's beast. She was ready to trust with her whole heart, ready to trust Kendrick.

He removed her black over-the-knee boots. He first pulled one off and then the next before kissing her ankles and arches as he slowly worked his magic. She had dressed with seduction in mind, and it seemed to have the desired effect on him. His hands moved to the zipper of her skinny black pants. She felt the slide of fabric as the pants slid down her hips. He tore them from her legs and flung them, along with the boots, across the room.

He circled her waist with his hands, lifted Aileana up, and tossed her to the middle of his sumptuous black-clad, king-sized bed. She landed on her back with a whoosh against his soft silky comforter. She'd never seen this side of her Selkie lover. His tangible lust ratcheted up her own raging libido.

Kendrick quickly removed his clothes and pounced on the bed, straddling her hips. He leaned down and tasted her lips. Aileana nipped at his full bottom lip before she sensed his tongue moving to explore her mouth as he sucked her plump bottom lip into his wet mouth. Their tongues fought for dominance; his mouth sucked at her tongue and pulled it into his mouth. He was out to conquer her last ounce of resistance, which hung by a slender thread.

Kendrick slid his huge body down as he dipped his head to nip at her inner thighs. His long, dark hair caressed her sensitive skin. His mouth moved to capture the moist inner folds between her legs. He lapped at her core; his tongue flicked her sensitive clit with the expertise and precision of a skilled lover. He took her to the edge of release and then eased back off, only to do it once again. Was he trying to make her lose what small amount of sanity she had left? She clawed at his head, gripped handfuls of his long hair to grind his face into her sex. She needed him to give her the fiery release that her body burned for.

His mouth gave exquisite pleasure and just the right amount of pain to the juncture between her thighs. His thumb pressed into her throbbing clit rubbing the sensitive button with a perfect pressure.

"Aileana, I crave yer sweetness now and will crave ye forever." He moaned with desire as he continued to feast at her pussy.

Down between her knees, Kendrick parted her legs wide over his thickly muscled shoulders to lie on his smooth brawny back. His obsidian eyes were fastened on her sex.

While he spoke so easily of his need, she felt a rush of wetness as she experienced the rumbling vibration of his voice against her. Aileana was totally engulfed with a rush of emotion for Kendrick. She decided to let her heart rule where her analytical mind was too afraid to go.

"Kendrick, I love you." There, she said it. *Wow.* She did it, she said it.

Kendrick stopped mid-stroke, his eyes met hers. "*Mo maise, tha gaol agam ort.*"

"Again! With the Gaelic? What did you say?"

"I said, mah beauty, I love ye," Kendrick stated.

"Kendrick, I do love you and have for quite some time. I was just too afraid to trust again. But your love has given me the courage to love again. I can't seem to get enough of you and your loving."

"Aye, lass, this is just the beginning of our loving, and sharing our life together. I also have a great need to be buried in yer wet folds." There was a wanton happiness in his voice.

"Let me show ye how pleasurable I can make it for the rest of our lives together."

With that smile on his face and his dark eyes blazing with his lust, he lowered his head again.

His tongue went back to probing her inner walls, and his fingers worked their magic against her throbbing clit. Within moments her world exploded with the pleasure of her orgasm.

Chapter 30

Kendrick

Aileana was still experiencing the strong rhythmic contractions of her intense orgasm. He moved up the bed to savor her beautiful full breasts. He plucked at her pert nipples with his mouth and let his teeth nip at them.

Kendrick lifted her off the bed and flipped her over on her stomach. Then, he raised her up on her knees with her beautiful arse in the air and her shoulders pressed into the mattress. He reached around and stroked her plump erect nipples. Her moans of pleasure drove him to the edge with his own need to release his seed into her sweet body. His inner animal wanted to take her and make her, his in every way. With his other hand, he stroked and pinched her swollen clit, using her abundant cream to prepare her for his entry. She writhed against his fingers, pushing to take his fingers deeper inside her tight hot channel. He stroked her beautiful firm arse with his thick cock between her sweet arse cheeks. Aileana pushed back against his hard shaft whimpering with the sounds of need. Above all else, she obviously wanted to be filled with his thick hard cock.

Her sex was drenched with her desire. He parted her silken thighs as he lifted his heavy member and placed it at her wet entrance. With one quick thrust, he was buried balls-deep in her lush body. This woman tested every ounce of control he had. The pleasure he received inside her wet snug channel nearly unmanned him. He felt the last waves of her strong orgasm as he entered her. He took a few deep breaths to regain his control. His thoughts shouted in his brain for him to *make her mine in every way now that he'd heard her words of love.*

He sought to draw out the pleasure so both would savor their next orgasm. He pushed his cock deeper into her cream-filled pussy, which was drenched with her desire to be taken and filled. Kendrick slowly withdrew to sliding all the way out. She had turned her beautiful face to the side and he watched her lush lips as she bit them with anticipation as he thrust back inside her tightness. This female was so hot with her desire she was on the verge of another orgasm. He continued with his strong, fast thrusts and his slow, prolonged withdrawal. He removed his fingers from stroking her sweet swollen clit as he drew her to the edge of her peak and reeled her back. He did this over and over, taking them both to the crest and backing off, to make their release that much more intense. Her channel's muscles gripped his cock in a nearly brutal clench. Her sweet young body worked hard to acquire what she desired above all else. What she wanted to possess more than anything at this moment was his cock to give her a sweet needed release.

With a thrust, he leaned over her smooth, silky back and renewed his attention to her swollen clit with firm rhythmic strokes that had her building back up to her pinnacle of desire. His body slid against her, his chest to groin caressed her from her arse to her shoulders. He brought his lips to the slender column of her neck and laved her with his tongue. As his teeth grazed the cords of her neck, she strained to reach her peak. Her body vibrated with the anticipation of her approaching release. His cock was gripped by the contractions of her explosive orgasm and flooded with her sweet-scented wetness. Her orgasm pushed him over the edge. As he came he bit her shoulder where it met her neck. He'd marked this woman as his territory for all to know; she was his alone. She let out a small yelp. He had drawn blood with this bite; he gently licked the few small drops of her blood from his final bonding bite.

She then turned her head back toward him and smiled as she whispered, "Payback is a bitch, Mr. Selkie, and you will get yours when you least expect it," she said with a voice still husky with her passion.

"Tis something I look forward to, *mo nighean ruadh*," he murmured in her ear. He gathered her up into his arms and wrapped his body tightly around hers. "Mah love, this is the sweetest homecoming a male could want. It was worth mah trip to the hospital to have ye give me what I wanted most."

"And, Mr. Selkie, what would that be, what could be possibly worth a trip to the hospital? And to have me worried out of my head for you?"

He rose up on his elbows and turned her face to his so that he could see into her emerald green eyes. "The words that bind us and make ye mine. Three small words that hold so much power over me and bring me more pleasure than I could have hoped fur." His mouth covered her sweet pouty lips with tender kisses.

"Oh, those three words." She smiled. "I love you and have for a long time. Only now, I am in love with you also. Do you understand?"

"*Aye, mo luaioh*, I understand the difference between the two. In the morning, I have much to discuss with ye."

"What, Mr. Selkie?"

"Dinna fash, it can wait until the morning. Now, we both need to rest so we may do this again in the morning," he said with a smile and pulled his life mate closer to his heart.

* * * *

After they spent a leisurely morning in bed playing all his favorite Selkie bed games, they enjoyed a shower together. Kendrick made breakfast while Aileana dressed for the day. He put together a hearty breakfast of oatmeal, a rasher of bacon, and bowls of fresh local berries with cream, to go with a pot of hot tea. While he prepared breakfast for them, he was going over in his mind what he needed to explain to her. There were some benefits of being a Selkie's life mate; he truly hoped she saw them as a benefit.

He sensed her as she approached the kitchen and wrapped her arms around him from behind. She snuggled against his back and gave a satisfied sigh.

He laughed. "You appear contented this morning."

"I feel happy and contented, thanks to you, Mr. Selkie. It's wonderful to see you planned to feed me after all our exercise between the sheets." She giggled.

"I needed to make sure ye kept up yer strength for all mah wicked plans for ye." He also was happy and content with all the pleasure they'd shared and knowing she loved him.

"Please take a seat and I will serve ye. If ye wouldn't mind grabbing the orange juice, it is in the fridge," he said.

"Everything smells yummy." She also eyed their morning feast.

"Do ye remember I mentioned there were some things I wanted to discuss with ye last night?"

"Yes, I remember, and you said it could wait until morning. What? Is something wrong?"

"Nay, nothing is wrong. There are some side effects of having a long-term Selkie lover that I wanted to make ye aware of." He gave her his best smile to reassure her.

"Now you're making me nervous with the smiles and all. What are you hiding from me? Am I going to sprout fins or develop a furry body?" she joked.

"Well...nothing quite so drastic."

"What then?" Worry was evident in her voice.

"Yer aging process will virtually stop until yer around four hundred years old. Then, ye will start aging again until we pass on from this life. That time frame is different fur each of us, same as in humans."

"How is it even possible? I'm not a Selkie!" she squeaked, a shocked expression on her face.

"That is the fun part of this conundrum." He smiled.

"Well, how about letting me in on this enigma of yours, Mr. Selkie?"

"It's about the exchange of our life essences. That exchange slows the aging process in the humans we mate with, or as ye might say, the exchange of bodily fluids."

"This only happens with a bonded life mate, otherwise a Selkie doesn't stay with a human long enough to make a difference."

"Is that the reason my *seanmhair* appears so much younger than most other seventy-year-old women?" she asked.

"I am sure that is part of the reason, yer *seanmhair* was only with yer Selkie grandfather around seventeen years before he died, correct?"

"The time frame sounds about right, from what my seanmhair has told me," she said.

"I would say between her excellent genetics and her age, which stopped fur the seventeen years they were together. That would be the apparent reason she appears much younger than most seventy-year-old women," he stated.

"Will my father not age at the regular human rate?"

"Nay, because he decided to give up his Selkie gift at a relatively young age and decided to be human, he will age as a normal human."

"It's a lot to take in. The part about the non-aging sounds good on the surface, but thinking about outliving everyone you love doesn't," she said.

"Everyone does die eventually, Aileana. Ye kin never predict who will live longer than ye will, and this is true fur

Selkies and humans alike. But when ye have yer own children they will make the passing of others less painful."

"But what if our children don't become Selkies? You told me there is only about a fifty percent chance of children becoming Selkies when there is only one parent which is human."

"Since I am full blooded and from the royal family our children will be Selkie. That is how it has always been through the generations. The royal family only has Selkie children when they are with their bonded life mate. It makes it possible to continue the royal line and allow a human life mate if that is who yer destined life mate is."

"I understand. You keep springing new surprises on me. How do you explain never getting older to the people you live around and work with?"

"That is a tricky problem. We move to different areas every fifteen to twenty years. And start over in the human world. All our homes and such are in a business account, so to all the humans that look into our records, it just shows a corporation name. We all enjoy several homes in different areas with a few assorted names."

"It all seems a little confusing right now. I'm sure I will get used to the idea and be able to wrap my brain around the whole concept. This is a lot of info to process before noon time," she stated.

"Yer going to be okay with all this and I will make ye happy with nay regrets for a different path," he stated.

"Okay, dude, I will trust my Mr. Selkie." She laughed.

Chapter 31

Aileana

Time had flown by since the night Kendrick shared his information with her about the extended lifespan of Selkies and their life mates. She guessed nature had to devise a way for a non-Selkie life mate to share the extra time their Selkie mate had on this planet. Her *seanmhair* knew all too well, there were no guarantees in the world of Selkies or humans. You needed to enjoy each day you're given and try to bring happiness to others.

She and Skye decorated a Christmas tree for their home. The tree gleamed with all *seanmhair's* beautiful ornaments she'd made or collected over the years. They'd put the tree up a week ago. They enjoyed a fine bottle of wine with crackers and cheese as they decorated the pine tree.

Skye gave Aileana some history on each of the ornaments. The oldest ornament on the tree was one Skye made of clay while in grade school. She told Aileana the whole class in primary school made an ornament they cut from rolled-out clay. Hers was in the shape of her pet duck. There was a small hole at the top of duck ornament with a ribbon attached to hang it on the tree. The duck ornament was at least sixty-five years old.

She also showed Aileana one which Iain her father made when he was in primary school. The teachers must have carried over the same tradition for the little ones from one year to the next. Her father's clay ornament was a seal he painted dark gray. The small seal ornament made perfect sense for the son of a Selkie.

Aileana enjoyed hearing the stories behind the ornaments, passing along stories and enjoying the time spent with family; it was part of what made the holidays so special. She had given a lot of thought into what she purchased for her family and Kendrick. She hoped they'd be pleased with her choices.

She sent her parents tickets for an Alaska cruise. They always talked about how much they wanted to make the trip but had never booked it. Now they would go at the end of the summer after their annual trip to Scotland.

For her sister, Aileana sent a beautiful dress for her to wear on New Year's Eve in Las Vegas. Adaira planned to go with her girlfriends to all the hottest nightclubs in town which they all enjoyed. It still amazed her that Adaira got her degree with excellent grades with all the clubbing she did.

For her *seanmhair*, she purchased a beautiful shawl of Sutherland plaid and a new pair of wellies for her to wear while she worked in the garden.

Aileana thought long and hard for the right gift for Kendrick. She'd placed an order a month back and just received the shipment a day ago. She purchased a surfboard so they'd be able to enjoy the waves together in human form. That didn't mean she wanted to give up her Selkie rides—that wasn't going to happen now. It was just too much fun to pass up now that she knew she could swim with the seals. But she wanted him to be able to enjoy surfing as much as she did.

The final gift to Kendrick was wrapped and under the tree at her *seanmhair's* cottage, waiting for him to open it after they ate their Christmas dinner. She looked forward to him joining her grandmother and her for the holiday dinner. This was her first Christmas in Scotland, and she enjoyed the festivities around town. Her only regret was not having her parents and sister here to celebrate the holidays with her in the highlands.

At least she would see her sister after the New Year. Aileana hoped whatever job Adaira interviewed for, it would work out for her. She liked the idea of having her in the same country as herself.

Christmas morning held the promise of turning into a beautiful day. She gave the roast Christmas goose it's final basting. The cut up apples and oranges that filled the bird's cavity gave the house a wonderful scent. She had just placed the goose back in the oven to continue roasting when she heard a knock at the front door.

"Aileana, I'll get the door," *Seanmhair* called from the living room.

"It's Kendrick, I'm sure," she replied.

Aileana overheard the greetings from the living room, *Seanmhair* wishing Kendrick a Merry Christmas. She couldn't catch much of their conversation. But she could hear her grandmother teasing Kendrick, and she could hear their laughter.

Kendrick stood in the kitchen doorway with two bottles of wine, one in each hand. He walked right up and wrapped his arms around Aileana. He pulled her in close to his chilled body for a wonderful, passionate kiss, still holding the bottles.

"That is the best way to warm a body up after the cold brisk walk here." He smiled at her with that wicked grin of his.

"I'm glad I am able to be so helpful!" She laughed.

"Merry Yule, *mo luaioh*," he said.

"Merry Christmas, Kendrick."

"Let's open a bottle of wine and have several of those tasty appetizers yer grandmother offered me as I walked in."

Aileana grabbed three wine glasses, along with a corkscrew, and followed Kendrick into the living room. He and her grandmother sat on the sofa facing the fireplace, which had a warm fire burning to keeping the cottage cozy. On one side of the fireplace was the Christmas tree with its colored lights glowing and the ornaments that brought thoughts of happy memories.

Kendrick poured their glasses full of the fragrant, full-bodied, old Bordeaux; a delightful red wine which paired well with the roasted Christmas goose. They sipped the wine as they sampled the smoked salmon with cream cheese and capers on toast points. Aileana put together a Holiday Brie en Croute loaded with dried cranberries and tasty apricot preserves. The pairings went well together; every sip and bite was tastier than the last. Her grandmother enjoyed the light hearted teasing Kendrick was giving her. Skye had met her match in the teasing department and there she'd thought she was the master. Aileana thought those years in Kendrick's long life must have made him the master of the fine art of lighthearted wit.

They cleared the dinner table and put away the leftovers. Afterward, they sat around the tree and opened packages. Skye opened her package from Aileana, carefully removing the silver ribbon that was wrapped around the flat box covered with red flocked paper.

"Aileana, the shawl is lovely, and the cashmere is velvety soft. I love that ye found our plaid. I will truly enjoy wearing the shawl," her grandmother said.

"Seanmhair, there's one more under the tree for you, from me."

"Which one is it, *mo brèagha?*" she asked.

"The large white wrapped package with the printed red bells on the paper," Aileana said.

"Aileana, ye shouldn't have bought so much! The shawl was more than plenty."

"*Seanmhair*, don't worry. This is our first Christmas together, and besides, I had fun shopping!"

"Och! Wellies! I needed new ones and these are so lovely and practical. I love the navy color with the flower print. They are perfect fur working in the garden. Yer such a sweet *ban-ogha*."

Seanmhair reached below the branches of the tree and pulled out a small package. The gift was wrapped in red paper with Santa Claus pictures embossed in white on the paper. She carefully placed the gift in Aileana's hand. She removed the ribbon and paper from the package. The gift was an old, worn, leather-bound book of Selkie tales. *Seanmhair* had subsequently told the story of the old book of Selkie legends. She had first received the book from her new husband, Mackenzie, on their wedding night. Her Mackenzie used the book to help her understand the story of his Selkie clan. He thought the book would be a way to help her with the knowledge he planned on sharing with his new bride.

Aileana had tears in her eyes that threatened to leak out at hearing such a beautiful story of her grandfather's love. Her *seanmhair* stated she wanted to pass the book down to her, now that she had her own Selkie love.

"I brought a gift fur ye, Skye," Kendrick said.

"Och! Ye shouldn't have, *balach*," Skye said.

A Selkie's Magic

He handed Skye a small wrapped package. She removed the ribbon and wrapping paper with care and beheld at a gorgeous book of Scottish folktales. She beamed at him and said she truly loved it. She told Kendrick the book happened to be one she didn't own and would make a wonderful addition to her collection.

Aileana told Kendrick to close his eyes and keep them closed until she told him to open them. He laughed and asked if his gift was too big to be under the tree. She told him to just keep his eyes closed and let her go get what Santa dropped off at their house for him. She went to her room and carried his gift with the big red bow on it back to the living room.

"Okay, you can open your eyes now."

"A surfboard fur me? Now I will be able to enjoy the waves more than one way," he said.

"We can go out together and surf. The surfboard will be for the times I don't take Selkie rides." She laughed.

"Aileana, as ye would say, I'm *stoked*, that *stick* is *totally sick*." He gave her his wicked grin.

"We'll have lots of fun together playing in the waves, Mr. Selkie," she said. "I have one more gift for you under the tree. It's that small box, the one with the green foil paper and the silver ribbon." She pointed to the one close to where he sat.

"Weel, that doesn't look like a wetsuit." He smiled.

"Silly man, Selkies don't need wetsuits."

He picked up the box and gave it a slight shake. It made a slight rattling noise as he shook it one way and then the other. He made silly guesses of what might be in the box. None of his the guesses were correct.

"You will just have to open it and see," she told him.

He tore the paper off in a flash and opened the black velvet box, only to stare at the pendant necklace she designed and had made up at a goldsmith's shop.

Chapter 32

Kendrick

Aileana never failed to surprise and please him. Her gift was perfect. He gazed at a stunning pendant necklace made in gold with a sturdy gold chain. The flat round disc was of a long-haired woman sitting on a surfboard, floating near rocks in the surf, a seal in the water close to the surfboard. The woman and the seal were looking at each other. The image was done in relief. Kendrick absolutely loved this pendant; he would wear it and always have a part of her close to his heart. He could wear it under his Selkie pelt. He would never have believed he would have received such a meaningful gift.

"Ye designed this? Ye had too, no one else would understand the true meaning of this piece of jewelry! I will wear it forever and have ye close to my heart always," he stated.

He was impatient to have her open his gifts to her. He placed the medium-sized box in her hands. The gift was wrapped in gold foil paper with seashells attached to the green ribbon tied around the package. She looked into his eyes and smiled.

"The box seems a little small to be a Harley of my own," she grinned.

"Och, ye dinna mean ye wanted a toy model of a Harley? I guess I misunderstood yer hints!" He laughed.

"Yeah, right, dude! I can't ride a toy! Besides, I wasn't hinting at any kind of gifts." She laughed along with him.

Aileana removed the paper wrapping from the gift and peered inside the box. Her eyes started tearing up again as she pulled out the carved wood sculpture of the stunning woman leaning back against a resting seal.

"Kendrick, it's us! Did you carve this?" she exclaimed.

"Aye, it is us, and aye, I made it for ye. I wanted something to remind ye of us when I am out on the oil platform working."

"It's a gorgeous piece of art that captures our essence perfectly. I'll treasure it always."

"Ye both were thinking the same thoughts when ye choose yer gifts to each other," Skye observed.

Aileana expressed to him how much she loved her gift; she reached over and threw her arms around his neck. She pulled him close to her face and let her sweet lips skim across his. He reacted in the way his body wanted. He pulled her closer and let his tongue glide across the seam of her mouth, till her lips opened to let his tongue slide inside. Kendrick felt himself rise to the occasion. He pulled her on his lap and placed her luscious bottom on top of his hard shaft. He thought her sweet grandmother didn't need to see what was going on in his lap, but she wasn't an eejit.

Kendrick murmured in her ear about the things he planned to do to her just as soon as they left her grandmother's home and were in his big bed. "Oh, Mr. Selkie, do tell." She laughed.

"Aileana, I have one more gift for ye."

He reached across to his leather jacket draped over the back of the sofa and pulled out a small wrapped package. She tore the paper off with childlike enthusiasm. She opened the blue velvet box and smiled as she viewed the pink teardrop-shaped pearl earrings he had the jeweler make for her. He'd wanted her to have earrings that matched the pearl he'd given her when they'd met.

"Kendrick, I love them, they're gorgeous. They'll look wonderful with my necklace."

"I had them set in a mounting to match the setting ye chose for the necklace. It means a lot to me to see ye wear the necklace. It is significant to me. I want to believe it must have meant something to ye. Otherwise, ye wouldn't have worn the pearl all this time since that summer we met."

"You have no idea how much meant to me. It was my first gift from a 'boyfriend.' That is what I always told myself. That you were my first boyfriend, even though we never even kissed."

"I knew ye were special, but I had no idea just how special ye would be to my life. Ye have to remember ye were just a young *cailin* at the time."

"Not so young. I noticed you were the hottest guy I'd ever seen."

"I like my women more mature than their teen years, but I knew even then that someday ye would be a stunning heartbreaker."

"Heartbreaker? Not me, that's something that is done to me."

"Weel, *mo chride*, this male will never break yer heart ever." He gazed into her eyes as he said the words.

Skye cleared her throat and asked if they would like dessert before she headed off to bed. "I made a Tipsy Laird Trifle fur dessert," she said.

"Skye, that sounds delicious, but I will have to pass tonight. I'm still stuffed from dinner, but maybe tomorrow I can sample your trifle."

"*Seanmhair*, I'm going to pass on dessert tonight. Kendrick and I are going on over to his cottage now."

Kisses and hugs were exchanged all around. They gathered up coats, mittens, and put on warm shoes for their walk to Kendrick's cottage.

* * * *

In the cottage he walked over to the hearth to stoke the fire, to chase the chill from the cottage. Next, he went to the kitchen and grabbed two highball glasses and the bottle of Highland Scotch. He thought they could use a bit of whiskey to warm them up until the fire warmed the room. He wanted to take the time and to enjoy every moment of their first of many holidays to come with each other.

Kendrick followed his woman into the bedroom and handed her one of the glasses of whiskey and said, "To us, mo chride," as he used his foot to push the bedroom door shut.

Chapter 33

Aileana

Kendrick made plans for their Hogmanay celebration. Hogmanay was what the Scots called New Year's Eve, the celebration of the last day of the year. The only thing he would tell her was that it was formal, and to pack a bag for a two-night stay. He definitely had a romantic streak. She wondered if that was a Selkie trait, or if it just him. She certainly wouldn't complain about his romantic inclinations.

She had a lovely midnight-blue silk georgette column dress picked out among her dressy clothes she'd brought from home. The floor-length gown had knee high slits on both sides, as well as an interesting cut-out in the back near the waist. The shoulders of the dress were cut-out with a high neckline. She planned on wearing her Stuart Weitzman Dizbebare heels that were a platinum color. She would look sexy and sophisticated.

She placed the gown in a garment bag and tucked the heels in the front zipped pockets of the bag. She'd already packed her other clothes for the trip. She brought a pair of Levi's, a Pendleton wool shirt, and a few sweaters since she didn't know what he planned for the rest of the trip. The gray wool dress pants tucked inside her black knee-high riding boots fit her perfect. On top, she wore a black cashmere turtleneck sweater with a black wool blazer. Aileana felt she'd covered all the contingencies of possibilities for what he may have planned.

She kept thinking about how he had been acting since Christmas, kind of twitchy. She sincerely hoped it had nothing to do with any new sighting of Finfolk. Even on

Boxing Day he seemed distracted as they went to the community center and gave out small gifts to the seniors.

She came up with an idea to do an article on the senior citizens. About their lives back when they were young and how living through World War II affected the people of this community. She was aware at the time of World War II, the area around Sango and Lerinbeg had operated as a top secret training facility. Durness had been an important link in coastal radar defense. The radar station was called RAF Sango. A few of the old buildings were still intact and used for other purposes at the present.

Well, maybe tomorrow she would approach Kendrick and ask what was making him so edgy. She didn't want to spoil their first New Year's Eve together, or as the Scots called it, Hogmanay.

Seanmhair had walked into the bedroom to let her know Kendrick was there and ready to go. She asked her grandmother if he'd dropped any hints where he planned to take them.

"Now if I told ye, it would ruin the boy's plans; ye will just have to find out fur yersel'."

"*Seanmhair*, you know me and surprises. I have no patience to wait to find out what my surprise is."

"Aileana, it looks like ye will just have to find a smidgen of that patience ye'v lost." She laughed.

"Big help you are, *Seanmhair*." She laughed along with her.

Chapter 34

Kendrick

On the short drive to Aileana's, he wondered how she would react to the surprise he planned to ring in the New Year. Kendrick decided he would surprise her with a three-day stay at Bunchrew House Hotel in Inverness. The Bunchrew was on the shores of the Beauly Firth. He had heard nothing but good reviews about the seventeenth-century Scottish mansion. The hotel had a four-star rating and the well-known restaurant, The Cedar Tree, had a Hogmanay gala six-course dinner planned with a *Cèilidh,* a traditional Gaelic gathering for singing and dancing.

The weather would be fair to slight drizzles for the time frame of their trip. The weather was an important factor in something Kendrick planned. No snow and fair weather played right into his plans for Hogmanay Eve. Even if the weather turned foul, he would still go through with his scheme; he'd just have to carry Aileana to the spot he wanted her.

Kendrick pulled up to Skye's cottage and jumped out of the car. He rapped on the front door. Skye answered his knock with a smiling face.

"Weel, balach, ye look like the cat that swallowed the canary. What do ye have planned?" Skye questioned him.

"Let's just say something special. I dinnae want to jinx it."

"Where are ye going? Can ye tell or nae tell me?" She smiled.

"Aye, I'm taking Aileana to Bunchrew House Hotel in Inverness."

"Och! Aileana should love that," Skye said with a gleam in her eye.

"That is the intent. I want this evening to be exceptional fur her; a night she'll always remember."

"I'll tell Aileana yer here. Ye'll need to get on yer way. What is it—close to a three-hour trip?"

"Aye, close to."

She went back to the bedrooms and he could hear her speaking to her granddaughter. Aileana and her grandmother both walked out carrying a suitcase each. Skye carried the small tote bag, and Aileana had the garment bag in her arms. It seemed as if she glowed; her bright smile lit up her beautiful face. His woman took his breath away; he just couldn't get enough of her. His insides were twisted in knots; he realized he would always feel love crazy in her presence. Those knots were knots of pleasure that made his blood race. His mind always went to the wild pleasure they shared.

"Let me carry the luggage," he said, to cover the evidence of his ever-present erection; at least while around Aileana.

Aileana said, "What a gentleman," as she eyed the front of his pants with a naughty smile on her face.

"I aim to please." He grinned back at her. "We need to get moving. We have a three-hour drive ahead of us."

Off they went in the car to start on their first Hogmanay holiday together.

"So, Kendrick, where are we headed?" she asked, trying to sound casual.

"*Mo luaioh*, wouldn't ye like to know?" he teased.

She laughed and replied, "Yes, I am not big on surprises."

"Ye will just have to wait and see! I will say we're heading south. Ye know the old proverb—patience is a virtue."

"Yeah, right, dude! Whatever." She smirked.

"I will tell ye, I thought we could go to one of the distilleries in the area, the day after the holiday if ye wish. There is a local distillery that makes the only remaining single malt scotch whiskey in the Black Isles."

"Well, now you're talking. That is a small hint of the area where we're traveling to! So the distillery is on the peninsula near Cromarty Firth to the north, the Beauly Firth to the south, and the Moray Firth to the east. I know which distillery you're referring to; I've done some research on Scottish whiskey. Ah ha! At least now I know the region, we're going," she said with glee.

"Aileana, ye are the most inquisitive woman I have ever run across. And that description almost sounded like something ye would write for yer magazine." He laughed.

"I just like to stay informed, all part of being a writer. Plus, Mr. Selkie, I do need to keep you on your toes," she said with a smile.

"That ye do, mo luaioh!"

"I forgot to mention to you, my sister plans to be in Scotland soon."

"She'll be here fur her holiday?" he asked.

"No, she said it was for a possible job."

"Where's the job, and doing what? Ye said she has her degree in geology, right?"

"She said she didn't want to tempt fate and say. So she wouldn't tell me anything more, other than to say she will be coming up to Durness to visit with *Seanmhair*. She's also looking forward to meeting you."

"Och, lass, that means ye'v told yer family back home aboot me."

"Well, I mentioned we bumped into each other and we are getting reacquainted."

He laughed and said something along the lines of, "Is that what they are now calling what we enjoy with each other?"

"I didn't want to overshare with them. What we do between the sheets or on the picnic blankets or on the fur rug in front of your fireplace, stays between us," she stated with a smile on her face.

Kendrick just laughed and kept the smile plastered to his face as he continued the drive to their destination.

"I don't know if I mentioned it to ye or not, but Duncan's spending his holiday time in yer home state," he said.

"Really! How did it happen that you didn't mention it to me? He could have gone and met my family if he was in the Los Angeles area."

"Och, did ye actually want him anywhere near yer sister! Ye know what a hell-raiser and womanizer he is."

"Well, when you put it that way, I guess you're right."

"Ah thought it best nae mention it to ye fur just that reason."

"I am sure my sister is not his usual target—oops, did I say target? I meant woman. Your brother and my sister would be like oil and water trying to mix. Scratch that, make it gasoline and a blowtorch. They're definitely not a good combo. Your brother's smoking hot, but she is not into the tatted-up, pierced, bad, boy, biker sort normally, only when she is in her rebellious mode. She generally likes her men on the fast-track to the top of the corporate food chain. You know the kind, all *GQ* and buttoned down." She laughed.

"So, *mo chride*, ye think mah brother's smoking hot?'

"Well, yes, he is hot in that tattooed, bad boy, biker way. But I'm in love with the extremely handsome, Selkie Morgan brother that is perfect for me." She smiled at him.

"I needed to check that yer sure yer with the correct Selkie brother." He smiled in return.

Chapter 35

Aileana

After close to three hours on the road, they pulled up in front of a beautiful old mansion that had been converted into a luxury hotel. It had a beautiful view, right on the shores of the Beauly Firth. The grounds were impressive. They'd arrived in time for the afternoon coffee and shortbread. The piping hot coffee and the shortbread were just what she needed to hold her over until the dinner hour.

Kendrick said they had time to take in the gardens. As they walked and viewed the gardens, he had tucked her under his arm. He kept her pulled up tight to his large warm body, close enough to feel the beat of his heart. She was secure in her love with this Selkie man, and she was content to be wrapped in his warm embrace. She felt a happiness she'd never before experienced and wouldn't have believed possible.

After they walked along the shore and spotted a few dolphins playing in the firth, they were also able to see the Kessock Bridge from the lawn of the hotel. They then decided to head back to the room to dress for the dinner party that the hotel planned for the holiday.

She moved to the bathroom and got ready in there. Kendrick would get ready in the bedroom. She was excited about the evening. This would be the first time he would see her in evening attire. She wore a little more makeup than she normally did, but she still kept the makeup on the natural side. Her one concession on the makeup would be going with the smoky eyes, which intensified the dark green of her eyes.

She tried to tame her long mane of soft curling auburn hair, deciding to style it in a half-up, half-down hairdo, using a few well-placed jeweled hair clips. She was pleased with her efforts, her hair looked softly sensual. Not too bad for a girl used to wearing her hair in a ponytail.

Before she slipped the gown on, she used a few spritzes of Eternity perfume. The perfume always put her in a special place. She knew it sounded strange, whether that was true or not, but that was how she felt when she wore the fragrance. It made her feel sensual. The gown had the touch of soft gossamer, virtually a fluid feeling. The silk floated down and around her lush curves while the gown wrapped around her in a subtle seduction of pleasure.

One last look in the mirror and she was ready to enjoy the dinner and festivities the hotel had planned. She opened the door and saw the most attractive male standing in the room. Kendrick wore a formal kilt outfit, from his black bowtie to his Ghillie Brogue's long laces which wrapped around his well-muscled legs to just below his calves. His ivory-colored kilt hose held an old world stag antler *sgian-dubh* in his right kilt hose.

Aileana slowly brought her eyes up to fall upon his badger sporran, which had sterling cantles trimming the top of the pouch. The sterling cantles were etched with Celtic knots and inlaid stones. The sporran appeared to be a family heirloom. The handcrafted sporran had undoubtedly been passed down through the generations of the clan Morgan. To finish off his formal attire, he wore the black wool Prince Charlie jacket and vest with the blue Morgan plaid kilt.

He was the most scrumptious vision of a male she'd ever seen. His virile, muscular body would make all women with a heartbeat swoon with desire to be in the same room with him. His long dark hair was pulled back into a queue tied with a length of black leather. As she approached him she became aware of his natural crisp spicy scent.

She thought, *Oh, dude, did it just get twenty degrees warmer in this room? Or did I just have a hot flash at the ripe old age of twenty-six, soon to be twenty-seven? Well, whatever it is, I am one extremely fortunate woman to have this man in love with me.*

"Aileana, ye are a lovely vision. I am the luckiest male in Scotland. I may need to use *mah sgian-dubh* just to fight the other males off ye," he said with a breathlessness to his voice.

"There will be no fighting males off of any sort tonight, I only have eyes for my Selkie." She laughed. "But I will undoubtedly need your *sgian-dubh* to ward off the women from trying to have their way with you."

"Nay, I also only have eyes, fur ye, *mo luaioh*."

"Mr. Selkie, you need not worry about me. No one in this world could budge me from your side."

"Shall we go downstairs to dinner? By the way, I will enjoy watching the other males' reaction to seeing yer beauty, especially knowing yer mine." His eyes were full of lust.

He opened the door of their suite, placed an arm around her waist and whispered in her ear, "I'm truly blessed to have ye in mah life and I will always cherish ye."

With his lips so close, she turned her head and brought her lips to his for a passionate kiss. She told him they were both fortunate to have found each other after their lips parted.

They walked arm in arm into the hotel dining room. The tables were set with snow-white linen and crystal stemware. The candles were all lit and gave the room a soft, warm glow of romance. She felt she'd walked into a wonderful dream world. The other guests barely registered in her mind. She felt they were in their own private world. Her senses were overwhelmed by the male that had her on his arm.

They enjoyed the most delightful meal, which was superb from the presentation to the delectable fresh cuisine. There were pipers and dancers to entertain, which all the guests enjoyed. After the entertainment, they had everyone dancing to a traditional Scottish band. She danced and danced until she thought her feet would give out.

Just before midnight, Kendrick said, "Let's take a short walk. The evening is brisk but clear. I would like to have ye all to myself at the stroke of midnight."

"That sounds fantastic. I would like a little fresh air. I am warm from all the dancing, and being within your sphere." She smiled.

"Aye, Aileana, ye have the same effect on me."

They proceeded out the front door and down a small walkway to where there stood a large old cedar tree. He pulled her into his arms and kissed her neck and whispered to her. "This old tree was planted before the battle of Culloden. It's recognized in the Highlands as a lucky tree."

"What type of luck does it bring, Kendrick?"

"That is why I asked ye outside, to tell ye aboot the luck that is made under this tree," he said solemnly. "It's identified as the 'Loving Tree' and known fur bringing good luck to all couples that get married beneath the branches," he stated.

Kendrick dropped to one knee and pulled out a small dark blue leather box. Aileana's heart started to pound. It was ready to jump out of her chest when she realized what he was about to do.

"Aileana, will ye do this Selkie the honor of becoming mah life mate for as long as we shall live?" He smiled. "I promise to keep ye happy and well-loved forever." His eyes gleamed with passion and promise.

"Yes, yes, I would be honored to be your life mate."

"Aileana, ye have made me happier than I could've ever wished. Ye will be the most loved and cherished woman forever and I will start to prove it to ye just as soon as we get back to our room," he promised.

"How could I say anything but yes after you've promised to keep me well-loved and happy?"

He reached for her hand and placed the gorgeous heart-shaped diamond ring on her finger.

Chapter 36

Kendrick

After Kendrick placed the heart-shaped diamond ring on Aileana's finger, he stood and wrapped her in his arms. He leaned down to cover her lips with his and her sweet lips parted for his probing tongue to taste her. He was now positive he was the happiest Selkie on the planet. As they sealed their commitment to each other, they heard fireworks and horns announcing the start of a new year. For them, this was the beginning of their new life together. He felt what he and Aileana had together would be the same joy his parents shared in their life together. With this fierce woman at his side, he knew the future of their Selkie clan would be strengthened.

Kendrick reached down and lifted her into his arms and carried her back to the hotel. As he bounded up the stairs to their room, he greeted fellow revelers with the words, "She said yes!"

Shouts of *"Congratulations"* and *"Happy New Years"* followed them till they were behind the doors of their suite.

He sat Aileana down on the bed and lifted her feet to remove her high-heeled sandals. He kissed each foot as he removed her heels. He took her hands and pulled her off the bed to stand so he could remove her evening gown. The gown floated down her body to the floor in a filmy blue puddle at her feet. He unhooked her black lacy strapless bra and hooked his fingers into the elastic at the sides of her tiny black lace panties. As he slid them down her smooth silky legs, he kissed the sweet spot where her legs met her body. She moaned softly as she threaded her fingers through his hair and pulled him to her mons.

Her scent was intoxicating, like a drug he just couldn't get enough of. He moved her to sit on the edge of the bed. There he knelt in front of her and gripped her thighs to spread her open. He placed his body between her thighs and viewed her wet glistening sex before dipping his head to taste her body's sweet nectar. His tongue delved inside her lush core, needing to give her satisfaction to get her ready to plunge his cock into her tight body. His tongue lapped at her moist folds and probed her internal ridges; all the while his thumb circled her swollen clit.

"Kendrick, please, I can't wait." She moaned.

Her head thrashed from one side to the other as she begged for her release. He let her know she would soon delight in her release, just not yet.

"Soon, mah bonnie lass, ye will have me inside ye, and ye'll have yer release the like's ye'v never imagined."

Kendrick moved his mouth from her clit to the inside of her thigh. He curved his middle finger, then slid inside her warm, welcoming body and rubbed the raised ridge of her G-spot. His finger stroked the ridges inside her body as his thumb swirled around her swollen clit. Her body pulsed as she climbed closer to her climax. The next moment he felt the rhythmic clenching of her body around his fingers buried deep inside her; he bit down on the inside of her tender thigh, marking her again for her pleasure and as his life mate.

While her body shuddered with the pleasure of her orgasm, he stood and raised her from the bed. Her legs wrapped around his large body and pulled him tight to her. Kendrick slid the head of his cock along her warm wet folds. His cock throbbed with the need to be inside her body. As he thrust up and set his cock deep within her body, he sat back down on the edge of their bed. He heard her soft whimpers of pleasure as he rocked their bodies back and forth. He held her upright in his arms and watched as the pleasure glowed in her eyes as their joining consumed them. Their mouths slid against each other's; she opened to his probing tongue to let him taste her. His hands slid along her silky smooth back and pulled her arse down hard against his cock.

The thought that she would be his for a lifetime was enough for him to use his Selkie magic to bind them together forever. This woman had committed to being his, which was all he needed to understand. Now, he would let his seed flow and hope that the creator of all life would see fit to bless them with a new life. That one of his swimmers would take hold in her womb and let them become parents to the next generation of Selkie rulers.

With these thoughts in Kendrick's head and heart, he plunged deep into the woman of his heart. And once again felt her body tighten around his shaft on the verge of her release. As he felt her silky, hot body clinch with her release around his cock, he reached his own pinnacle and felt his body explode with its own release.

The End

Gaelic Glossary—Scottish (S)

Aboot (S)—about

a leannan—sweetheart

Aon—one

Athair –Father

Aye (S)—yes

Ban-ogha—granddaughter

Bairn/wean (S)—baby/ child

Balach-boy or lad

Bhalaich—boy

Bheag—little

Bothy (S)—small shack or hut

Brèagha—grand, lovely, pretty

Cailin (S)—girl

Cèilidh—is a traditional Gaelic social gathering, which usually involves playing Gaelic folk,

Music and dancing.

Cannae (S) – can not

Coudnae (S)—couldn't

Creag—rock, cliff

Didnae (S)—Didn't

Dinnae (S)—Don't

Dinna fash (S)-don't worry, don't be troubled

Fur (S)—for

Hogmanay (S)—is the Scots word for the last day of the year and is synonymous with the celebration of the New Year (Gregorian calendar) in the Scottish manner

Ken (S)—to know

Kin (S)—can

Loch (S)—lake

Mah (S)—my

Màthair—Mother

Mo chride—my heart

Mo luaioh—my beloved, darling

Mo maise—my beauty

Mo nighean—my lass or my girl

Mo nighean mhaiseach—my beautiful girl

Nae (S)—not

Nay (S)—no

Nighean ruadh—red hair girl

O bhalaich—O boy, is a form of address

Och! (S)—oh!

Ruaidh –red

Samhainn—is a Gaelic festival marking the end of the harvest season and the beginning of winter or the "darker half" of the year. It is celebrated from sunset on 31 October to sunset on 1 November.

Seanmhair—grandmother

Sgian-dubh—is a small, single-edged knife (Gaelic sgian) worn as part of traditional Scottish Highland dress along with the kilt.

Tha gaol agam ort—I love you

Verra (S)—very

Weel (S)—well

Ye (S)—you

Yer (S)—your

Ye'v (S)—you'll or you've

Yersel' (S)—Yourself

A Selkie's Magic

Glossary of Surfer terms

Ankle Busters— Small waves.

Anglin'— Turning left and/or right on a wave.

Bail, Bail out—to abandon or ditch one's surfboard before getting wiped out by the wave, either paddling out, or while riding the wave.

Bogus— False; lame; ridiculous; unbelievable

Dude— not strictly speaking only a surfing term, but for years this was the only place it was used. Strangely enough, the word originally meant a tramp /scarecrow

Dawn patrol— literally going surfing at dawn. An early morning surf session before sunrise. This time usually offers the least crowded and cleanest conditions before the winds pick up

Epic— Excellent, An adjective to describe an excellent surf session, a great wave, etc. Example: "how was it yesterday? Ah, dude, it was epic!"

Fer Sure— the surfer pronunciation of "for sure," meaning absolutely, correct, or definitely.

Goofy foot— if you stand with your right foot forward you are a goofy footer!

Gnarly— Excellent, really great

Grommet— A young hodad; a beginning surfer

Leash— the leg rope that connects a surfer to their board. Invented by Pat O'Neill in 1971

Lana Lea Short

Mavericks— this is a famous big wave spot off the California coast.

Men in Grey Suits-- SHARKS!

Outside Break— the area farthest from shore where the waves are breaking.

Pendleton— A brightly colored plaid wool or flannel shirt worn by some surfers.

Pop-up— getting to one's feet, after catching the wave.

Radical / Rad— High performance or risk taking surfing, awesome or impressive

Rail— the side of the surfboard and the part you are supposed to turn on. Can either be soft (rounded) or hard (angular)

Sand Facial— the result of wiping out and being dragged along the bottom, face first.

Set— Waves like to travel in groups. The exact science isn't understood but they tend to arrive in anything from 2 to what seems like infinity if you are paddling out!

Sick— a term used to describe when someone does something impressive, e.g. "that was a sick air"—not just because you have swallowed too much sea water

Sketchy— the opposite of surfing smoothly with style

Shortboard— a small surfboard.

Steamer— A wetsuit with long arms and long legs

Stick— a surfboard

Stoked— to be pleased

Takeoff— the start of a ride.

Unreal— Excellent, incredibly good.

Wax— Surf Wax is made from paraffin, colors and other additives and is put on your board to help you grip to it and not fall off while surfing because it does get slippery once you get your board in the water. Wax is the only thing that will help you stick to your board!

Wedge, The— A famous, but dangerous, body surfing spot located at the tip of the Balboa Peninsula in Newport Beach, California.

Worked— get pounded by a wave. To "get worked" is to wipe out and get thrown about while being held under by the wave. California Term

The 405— is a freeway from the San Fernando Valley to the beach in Southern California. Rush hour is like a parking lot instead of a freeway.

Lana Lea Short

ABOUT THE AUTHOR

Lana Lea Short, I am a paranormal romance writer. Born and raised in Southern California. Reading is my guilty pleasure, I've been a book addict since the age of eight. When I'm not reading I enjoy gardening, cooking and Texas Hold'em Poker. I'm married to a wonderful husband who lets me be me, though he may not totally understand his wife's crazy ways. I enjoy writing about strong, smart and loving women, who happen to show their softer side when it suits them and the alpha males they're drawn to.

Made in the USA
Lexington, KY
18 February 2017